GUINEA-PIGS IN THE GREENHOUSE

Mandy stared round in horror. Hutches had been overturned, splintered and cracked where they had been trampled on. Here and there, she spotted guinea-pigs amid the mess; small groups cowering in corners, or bolder individuals chomping lazily on the scattered hay.

Mrs Woodbridge bent down and scooped up a small dark shape in both hands. 'It's Abby!' she whispered happily, looking closely at the trembling guinea-pig. 'Scared half to death, but apart from that she seems all right.'

'Thank goodness,' Mandy whispered back. 'But where's Chocky?'

Animal Ark series

1 Kittens in the Kitchen
2 Pony in the Porch
3 Puppies in the Pantry
4 Goat in the Garden
5 Hedgehogs in the Hall
6 Badger in the Basement
7 Cub in the Cupboard
8 Piglet in a Playpen
9 Owl in the Office
10 Lamb in the Laundry
11 Bunnies in the Bathroom
12 Donkey on the Doorstep
13 Hamster in a Hamper
14 Goose on the Loose
15 Calf in the Cottage
16 Koalas in a Crisis
17 Wombat in the Wild
18 Roo on the Rock
19 Squirrels in the School
20 Guinea-pig in the Garage
21 Fawn in the Forest
22 Shetland in the Shed
23 Swan in the Swim
24 Lion by the Lake
25 Elephants in the East
26 Monkeys on the Mountain
27 Dog at the Door
28 Foals in the Field
29 Sheep at the Show
30 Racoons on the Roof
31 Dolphin in the Deep
32 Bears in the Barn
33 Otter in the Outhouse
34 Whale in the Waves
35 Hound at the Hospital
36 Rabbits on the Run
37 Horse in the House
38 Panda in the Park
39 Tiger on the Track
40 Gorilla in the Glade
41 Tabby in the Tub
42 Chinchilla up the Chimney
43 Puppy in a Puddle
44 Leopard at the Lodge
45 Giraffe in a Jam
46 Hippo in a Hole
47 Foxes on the Farm
48 Badgers by the Bridge
49 Deer on the Drive
50 Animals in the Ark
51 Mare in the Meadow
52 Cats in the Caravan
53 Polars on the Path
54 Seals on the Sled
55 Husky in a Hut
56 Beagle in the Basket
57 Bunny on the Barge
58 Guinea-pigs in the Greenhouse

Plus:
Little Animal Ark
Animal Ark Pets
Animal Ark Hauntings
Animal Ark Holiday Specials

LUCY DANIELS

Guinea-pigs — in the — Greenhouse

Illustrations by Ann Baum

a division of Hodder Headline Limited

Special thanks to Stephen Cole

Thanks also to C. J. Hall, B.Vet.Med., M.R.C.V.S., for reviewing the veterinary information contained in this book.

First published in Great Britain in 2002
by Hodder Children's Books

For more information about Animal Ark,
please contact www.animalark.co.uk

10 9 8 7 6 5 4 3 2 1

A Catalogue record for this book is available from the British Library

ISBN 0 340 85113 9

Typeset by Avon Dataset Ltd, Bidford-on-Avon, Warks

Printed and bound in Great Britain by
Clays Ltd, St Ives plc

Hodder Children's Books
a division of Hodder Headline Limited
338 Euston Road
London NW1 3BH

One

'Got you!' cried Adam Hope in triumph.

Mandy Hope couldn't help laughing as Viking, the Angora goat, gave an indignant bleat. She and her father had herded him into the corner of his paddock. Now they just had to make sure he *stayed* there for a few minutes.

'Sorry, but it's for your own good,' Mandy told the shaggy animal. 'Even Vikings need their hooves trimmed!'

Mandy's parents owned a vet's practice called Animal Ark, in the Yorkshire village of

Welford. Today, Adam Hope had been called out to Woodbridge Farm Park, a working farm that was open to the public. Mandy often went along on calls with her mum and dad. She loved animals, and spent every moment she could with them. One day, Mandy intended to be a vet herself.

Mr Hope struggled to keep hold of the goat's hoof in one hand while he reached for his trimmers.

'You'd better be quick, Dad,' Mandy said, as the goat shifted about restlessly.

'It won't hurt, Viking,' said Adam Hope in a soothing voice as he picked up the trimmers and set to work.

Mandy could see how Viking had got his name. He had amazing horns that curled out on either side of his shaggy head, just like the horns on a Viking helmet. Mandy ran her fingers through the soft tangles of wool that covered the goat's body, trying to calm him. Viking bleated again, but more quietly this time.

'That's good, Mandy,' said Adam Hope, clipping quickly at the hoof. 'See how these hard deposits have built up? I'll get them off much faster if Viking keeps still.'

Mandy watched as her dad worked at the walls of the hoof.

'We want a nice flat sole with no dirty pockets,' he explained.

Viking grunted, as if he thought his hooves were flat enough already. Mandy gave his warm flank another stroke. 'It won't be long now, Viking,' she promised.

The goat behaved himself for the rest of the trimming, and soon Mr Hope was packing away his tools. 'All done,' he told Viking as he stood back up.

'Where to now, Dad?' asked Mandy as they let the goat trot happily away in his paddock.

Mr Hope grinned. 'Pets' Corner,' he said. 'One of Mr Woodbridge's guinea-pigs is "in-pig", and he wants to be sure she's OK.'

Mandy frowned. 'In-pig?' she echoed. Then a smile spread over her face. 'You mean she's pregnant! There are guinea-piglets on the way!'

'Well, they're not really piglets,' Mr Hope told her. 'They tend to be called babies.'

'Oh well,' Mandy said. 'Whatever they're called, I bet they'll be adorable!'

They set off for Pets' Corner. A narrow path with hedgerows on either side led down from the paddock to a courtyard that had been converted into the visitors' picnic area. Low stone barns bordered the courtyard. Chairs carved from tree trunks were placed neatly beside wooden tables, awaiting the first customers of the day.

Mandy felt the early morning sun on the back of her neck. It was surprisingly warm for September. She had to keep reminding herself that the summer holidays were nearly over and that autumn was on its way.

Just then, a voice called across from one of the barns. 'Hey, Mandy!'

Mandy looked over in surprise. A short, stocky boy with close-cropped hair was waving to her.

'Dillon!' Mandy exclaimed. 'Hi! How are you?' She turned to her dad. 'Dillon's in my class.'

'He's pretty keen to be down here so early,' Mr Hope remarked.

'He is,' Mandy told him. 'He loves animals.' Not many people had realised that when Dillon was younger – not even Mandy. In fact, Dillon Lewis had been regarded as a bit of a bully. He'd kept the fact that he cared about animals secret, in case people thought he was soft. It was only when he met a lamb called Snowy, right here at Woodbridge Farm Park, that people began to see that Dillon wasn't such a bully after all.

'What are you doing here?' Mandy asked.

'I'm helping my brother out for the summer,' he replied.

'Of course, Gary works here full-time, doesn't he?' said Mr Hope. 'He's great with the animals.' He smiled and held out his hand. 'Pleased to meet you, Dillon.'

Dillon shook Mr Hope's hand, grinning, then turned to Mandy. 'I've just been cleaning out the rabbit hutches in Pets' Corner. Do you want to help me put the rabbits back inside?'

'I'd love to,' Mandy replied. 'But Dad's got to examine a pregnant guinea-pig, and I'm dying to see her too.'

Dillon's smile became wider. 'You mean Chocky! Come on, I'll show you where she lives.'

He led them into the barn. It was light and airy, and smelled sweetly of hay and sawdust. It was a lovely home for rabbits and guinea-pigs. Little peeps, squeaks and murmurs went up from the roomy hutches and pens as they walked through. The animals were all sorts of colours, from snow-white through to chocolate-brown. Some were scampering about, nibbling seeds or leaves, while others sat very still, watching the visitors intently.

'Chocky's over here,' Dillon told them, gesturing to one of the hutches. 'She lives with another guinea-pig called Abby.'

Mandy peered inside. The hutch was divided into two rooms. There was a living space protected with wire mesh, and a sleeping area behind a wooden door, where the guinea-pigs could retreat if they felt like privacy. At first Mandy thought the guinea-pigs must be sleeping. Then she spied a tiny twitching nose sticking out from the sleeping area.

Dillon made a soft clicking noise with his tongue. 'Come on, girl,' he said. 'Come and see us.'

Slowly, the guinea-pig edged forward into the light. She had brown and white fur which lay in perfect circular rosettes. Her eyes were wide and black, and her ears were smooth and thin like pink felt. But the most striking thing about this guinea-pig was her enormous size! She waddled out into the living area, her swollen stomach rubbing against the clean sawdust Dillon had just put down.

'Unless Abby's been eating too many sunflower seeds, this must be Chocky!' Adam Hope said with a smile.

Mandy nodded in agreement. 'She's huge!'

'She's doubled in size over the last two months,' Dillon told her.

Mandy shook her head in wonder. 'How many babies is she going to have?'

'Litters vary from just one baby to as many as six,' said Adam Hope, opening the hutch door. 'Chocky's so big because guinea-pig babies are born very well-developed.'

Mandy and Dillon watched as Mr Hope reached in with both hands. With one hand supporting her rump and the other placed under her forelegs, he splayed out his fingers to ensure Chocky's belly was well supported. Then he gently lifted her out of the hutch. 'Let's have a look at you then,' he murmured. 'Mandy, Dillon, could you get me some more light?'

Mandy took an electric lantern from its hook on a wooden beam above them. Dillon uncoiled the cable and switched it on for her. Mr Hope started to examine the guinea-pig.

'Quite a crowd in here for this time of the morning!' came a cheery voice from behind them.

Mandy turned to see Mr Woodbridge striding into the barn. He was a tall man whose friendly face was ruddy from a life spent working outdoors. His green overcoat matched his wellington boots, and he touched his cap to Dillon and Mandy in welcome. 'Viking seems pleased with his nice trimmed feet. Now, how's my little pig doing?'

'She's fine, Stuart,' Adam Hope called over.

'Good, good.' The farmer smiled with relief. 'I've been feeding her the raspberry leaf tablets you gave me, one a day, just as you said.'

'What are they?' Mandy wondered.

'They're like a vitamin supplement,' Adam Hope replied.

'I don't like to take chances with the little ones when they're pregnant,' Mr Woodbridge explained, and Mandy smiled.

'Well, there's not long to wait now till the big day,' said Adam Hope as he carefully brought Chocky a little closer to Mandy and Dillon. 'Can you see the way her pelvic bones have widened?'

Mandy peered at the guinea-pig's hindquarters. 'I think so,' she said.

'That means she's getting ready for the birth,'

her dad went on. 'I reckon the babies will be coming in the next 48 hours!'

'Will they have good homes?' Mandy asked Mr Woodbridge anxiously.

'Don't you worry,' Mr Woodbridge told her. 'They'll be staying right here with their mother!'

Just then they heard urgent squeaking from Chocky's enclosure.

'Uh-oh,' said Dillon. 'Abby's noticed her friend's missing. She must be getting worried!'

Mandy crouched down to look as Dillon scooped up the noisy guinea-pig. Abby's smooth, straight fur was all one colour, a deep warm brown. As Dillon stroked her, she soon quietened down.

'You should enjoy the peace and quiet while you can, Abby,' Mandy told her with a big grin. 'In a couple of days you won't be able to move for baby guinea-pigs!'

Carefully, Adam Hope placed Chocky back in her enclosure. She shuffled off and started eating a piece of juicy cucumber.

'You'll need to keep an eye on her, Stuart,' said Mr Hope, 'but I don't think you've got much to worry about so long as she's kept calm and secure.

Most guinea-pig births go without a hitch, as you know.'

Mr Woodbridge nodded. 'And usually at night. First thing we know about a new litter is when we see the little ones running about the next morning!'

As Chocky waddled back into the sleeping area, Dillon put Abby back inside, too.

'Can I come back and see the babies when they're born?' Mandy asked.

Mr Woodbridge chuckled. 'Of course you can. Why don't you bring some dandelion leaves or groundsel for Chocky? Next to cucumber, they're her favourite things to eat. And I reckon she'll have earned a treat after bringing her babies into the world.'

Mandy grinned. 'I'll bring as much as I can find.'

'I could do with some food, too,' said Mr Woodbridge, his eyes twinkling. 'Can I interest anyone in some morning coffee?'

'Consider me very interested,' smiled Mr Hope, winking at Mandy and Dillon.

'If it's all right, I'd like to look round a bit more,' Mandy said.

'Of course it's all right, Mandy,' said Mr Woodbridge.

'Hey, Mandy,' said Dillon. 'Do you want to see Snowy? You won't believe how much she's grown!'

Mandy smiled at the thought of the lamb that had helped the two of them become friends. 'That would be great,' she said. 'And we can look out for dandelion leaves and groundsel on the way!'

The morning sky was a deepening blue, scattered with puffy white clouds. It was going to be a lovely day. Dillon led Mandy across the courtyard and up the path to the upper field. Soon they came to a gate set in a dry stone wall. On the other side, a flock of about two dozen sheep and lambs were gathered around a long, shallow trough, eating some sheep nuts. There was a friendly-looking woman watching them.

'Hi, Mrs Woodbridge,' called Dillon, and Mandy waved.

'Hello, Dillon,' said Mrs Woodbridge, 'and hello, Mandy. I wondered if you'd come visiting with your dad.'

Mandy nodded. Just then, a large, stocky sheep

pushed her way out of the flock and took a few cautious steps towards the gate.

'Snowy!' Dillon cried. 'How are you, girl?'

'That's Snowy?' Mandy gaped in surprise.

Dillon nodded. His face split into a grin of delight. 'I told you she'd grown. She's even got lambs of her own now.'

As if on cue, two little lambs tottered out of the flock and lolloped over to Snowy.

'Meet Snowdrop and Snowflake,' said Dillon happily.

'Lovely, aren't they?' chuckled Mrs Woodbridge. 'Well, now you've said hello to the sheep, how would you like to help me take them up the road to the smaller field? Molly's giving a demonstration later on this morning, and she's back home being groomed for the occasion.'

'Molly's the sheepdog,' Dillon explained.

'Then we'd love to,' Mandy grinned.

'Come on then!' said Mrs Woodbridge. She called to the sheep and they began to bundle through the gate after her, into the lane. Snowy was the last to leave the field, her lambs sticking close beside her.

'I'll lead the way,' Mrs Woodbridge announced. 'You follow on behind, and round up any stragglers!'

As Mandy and Dillon followed the fluffy queue of sheep out into the road, Mandy heard a distant roaring, getting louder. 'What's that?' she asked.

Dillon listened too. 'Sounds like motorbikes,' he replied. 'Quite a few of them.'

'Come on, you two,' Mrs Woodbridge called, clapping her hands. 'Keep up the pace! We're blocking the road!'

'You heard her,' Dillon told Snowdrop and Snowflake. 'Hurry up. Soon you'll be in a nice new field with plenty of fresh grass.'

The roaring of motorbike engines got louder. Mandy glanced over her shoulder and saw five bikers round the corner and screech noisily to a halt just behind them.

'Oh great,' moaned the biker leading the way. 'A roadblock! Just what we need.'

Mrs Woodbridge waved at Mandy and Dillon, urging them to keep the sheep moving.

'Come on!' called one of the other bikers. 'We've been up all night.'

'Anyone fancy lamb for breakfast?' jeered another.

'Yeah,' laughed the biker in front. 'Chop, chop, or it's lamb-chop time!'

'We won't be long,' Mandy told him coolly. 'We're just moving the sheep into the next field.'

The biker revved his engine. Snowdrop skittered nervously, and Mandy called to the lamb and shepherded her along as fast as she could. One of the other bikers shouted at them to hurry up.

'Don't make so much noise,' Dillon called back fiercely, glancing down at Snowy as he shooed her forwards.

'What's that, kid?' one of the bikers enquired lazily, revving his engine again. He grinned at his gang. 'Can't quite hear you.'

The others took this as a cue, and revved their own engines. Now Snowflake gave a high, worried bleat.

'I've had enough of this,' the biker's leader said suddenly. 'Come on!'

Before Mandy knew what was happening, the bikers started off again, pushing their way through the nervous sheep. Mandy and Dillon yelled at them to stop, but the only response they got was an apologetic shrug from the biker at the back as he passed Mandy. The sheep weren't happy at being so close to the noisy machines, and one of them started panicking and pushing its way back out of the flock.

'Watch out!' Dillon called to Mandy. 'That one's going to bolt for it!'

Mandy wasn't sure what she should do – if she tried to hang on to the sheep, she might scare it even more, but if she let it run past her it could be hit by traffic further up the road!

Luckily, before she had time to decide what to do, Snowy let out a stern bleat from the middle of the flock, as if she was telling the sheep to calm down. The panicking ewe skittered to a stop, and Mandy and Dillon were able to urge her back into the flock.

'No one messes with Snowy!' Dillon said proudly.

A few minutes later they ushered the last of the sheep into the next field. The growl of the motorbikes dwindled to a distant whine further up the lane.

Mrs Woodbridge mopped her brow and smiled at Mandy and Dillon. 'Well done, you two.' She swung the gate shut with a resounding thud. 'I don't know what those bikers were thinking of, scaring the sheep like that!'

'I haven't seen them round Welford before,' said Mandy, staring down the lane after them. 'But that one at the back . . .' She frowned.

'What is it, Mandy?' asked Dillon.

'It's the strangest feeling,' Mandy told him, thinking hard. 'But I'm sure I've seen that biker somewhere before!'

Two

The sheep soon settled into their new field, nibbling peacefully at the lush grass. Mrs Woodbridge wanted to stay for a while to clear the gate of nettles so there was no risk of Molly's audience getting stung later on. She thanked Mandy and Dillon, and with a cheery wave they walked back down the road.

'I wish I could remember where I've seen that boy before,' Mandy sighed. Then she stopped in her tracks.

'What is it?' asked Dillon. 'Have you remembered?'

'No, but look!' Mandy pointed at the grassy verge beside them. 'That's groundsel, isn't it? Let's pick some for Chocky!'

Dillon grinned at her as she grabbed huge clumps of the spindly yellow flowers. 'Looks like Chocky will be getting even bigger at this rate!' he joked.

Once they had gathered up several armfuls of groundsel, they headed back towards the farm. Mandy saw a tall boy in his late teens standing in the middle of the empty sheep field. As he turned round, Mandy realised it was Gary, Dillon's brother. He was tall and thin, and his long blond hair was pulled back in an untidy ponytail.

Gary saw them coming through the gate and waved. 'Hey, you two. Haven't seen a flock of sheep anywhere, have you?'

'Maybe,' Dillon called back. 'Why, have you lost one?'

'Any jokes about Little Bo Peep, Dillon,' Gary warned with a grin, 'and I'll chuck you in the sheep dip!'

'Sure,' Dillon laughed.

Mandy watched Gary walk over to join them. He'd been working here for a few years now and, like her dad said, he was great with all the animals. But when she'd first met Gary three years ago he'd acted like a real bully, teasing poor Snowy with a stick while his friend held the struggling lamb in the air. Dillon had stood up to the older boys and told them to stop being so stupid. In the end, Gary had realised Dillon was right, and had apologised.

'Hi, Mandy,' said Gary. 'Can *you* tell me about those sheep I'm supposed to be shifting, then?'

Mandy explained that she and Dillon had arrived in time to help Mrs Woodbridge, and told him what had happened as they'd herded the flock along the road.

Gary frowned when he heard about the bikers. 'Not very clever of them,' he mused. 'Still, they're probably long gone by now, and you two have saved me a job!' Then his face fell. 'Which means I'm free to go and clean out the pigsty!'

Dillon laughed. 'You should feel at home there. Mum's always saying your room's just like one!'

'Watch it, Shrimp,' Gary joked as he strode off. 'See you later!'

'It's funny to think that Gary used to tease you about liking animals,' Mandy said. 'He really loves his job, doesn't he?'

'Yeah, we get on much better now,' Dillon agreed. 'Of course, he's still a pain sometimes. Then again, he probably thinks I'm a pain, too.' He grinned. 'That's what brothers are for, I guess. Still, he's taught me loads about nature and wildlife, especially birds. They're his real passion.'

'It's great that you've got things in common,' said Mandy with a smile. 'Come on. Let's get back to Pets' Corner.' She brandished her clump of groundsel. 'We've got a special guinea-pig delivery to make!'

The groundsel went down well with all the guinea-pigs. Mandy started off by feeding it to Chocky, but the others made so many chirps and peeps as their little pink noses sniffed the fragrant plants, that she and Dillon were soon sharing the treats around. Chocky still ate more than any of the others, though, her sharp little teeth nibbling through the stems as fast as she could go.

'I'm not surprised she's hungry,' Mandy said, stroking the guinea-pig's head. 'She's probably eating for five or six.'

Just then, Mr Hope poked his head round the barn doorway. 'I've finished up here now, Mandy. Are you ready to go?'

Mandy nodded, and said goodbye to Dillon. 'Will you be here tomorrow?'

'You bet!' said Dillon. 'I'm keeping a close eye on Chocky, just in case her babies come early.'

'Well, I'm going to go looking for some dandelion leaves when I get home,' Mandy declared. 'I'll bring them tomorrow morning.'

'See you then!' grinned Dillon.

Mandy and her dad drove down the bumpy track leading from the farm park. 'Can you drop me off at James's house please, Dad?' she asked. Mandy's best friend, James Hunter, lived at the other end of Welford. 'I bet he'd like to help me search for Chocky's treats!'

'Sure,' answered Adam Hope. 'You know,

guinea-pigs are fond of lots of wild plants. Dock leaves, clover – not pink clover though – sow thistle . . .'

'I'm not sure I'd recognise a sow thistle,' Mandy admitted. 'What else?'

'Mallow, knapweed, yarrow, hawkweed . . .' Mr Hope pulled up outside James's house. 'But do try to leave some greenery in Welford, won't you?' he teased. 'And mind out for buttercups, they're poisonous to guinea-pigs. See you later!'

As her dad drove away, Mandy walked up the drive to James's house and rang the bell.

James opened the front door, his brown hair ruffled from sleep. 'Hi, Mandy!' he said with a yawn. 'You're round early, is everything OK?'

'Early? It's gone nine o'clock!' Mandy said. 'Everything's fine, I just thought you'd like to help me put together a guinea-pig food parcel.'

She couldn't help laughing at James's astonished expression. His glasses slipped right to the end of his nose.

Mandy explained about Chocky, and James beamed at her.

'Come inside,' he said. 'I'll get some bags for us

to carry the plants. And Blackie can help us look, too!'

'Are you training him as a sniffer dog now?' Mandy teased. Blackie was James's dog, a black Labrador, who was as adorable as he was disobedient.

A few minutes later, Blackie was on a lead and Mandy's jacket pockets were stuffed full of carrier bags. Then the party set off in search of tasty treats for Chocky.

Mandy and James foraged along the verges of Welford for the next few hours. Blackie kept pulling them onwards, straining at his lead and sniffing about as if he was searching too. The knees of their jeans were covered in grass stains and their legs ached from walking. But by the end of the long, warm morning they had one bag full of dandelion leaves and another two filled with a mixture of groundsel, yarrow and chickweed.

'Let's take a break,' James suggested, wiping his brow as they leaned against the oak tree in the middle of the village green.

'But we haven't tried the car park at the Fox and Goose yet,' Mandy said brightly, pointing down the road. 'There are always weeds round the edges there.'

'Don't let Sara Harding hear you say that,' James told her with a grin. 'She might not let us in.'

They walked on down the road. As they neared the pub, Mandy heard the approaching roar of motorbike engines. 'Here they are again,' Mandy groaned as five familiar bikers came into view. 'You won't believe it, but those bikers rode right through the sheep this morning!' she explained to James.

The bikers roared past them and slowed down outside the pub. Mandy noticed that some of the people enjoying a drink in the garden looked round in annoyance as the lads pulled up. One of the pub's customers was Sam Western, a stocky man with carefully combed grey-blond hair. He was the richest farmer in the district and owned Upper Welford Hall. He scowled as the bikers began to prop their bikes on stands and dismount.

'Hey, isn't that Gary Lewis?' James pointed to a pony-tailed figure crossing the pub garden with a tray of drinks.

'Yes, it is.' Mandy watched Gary walk over to a

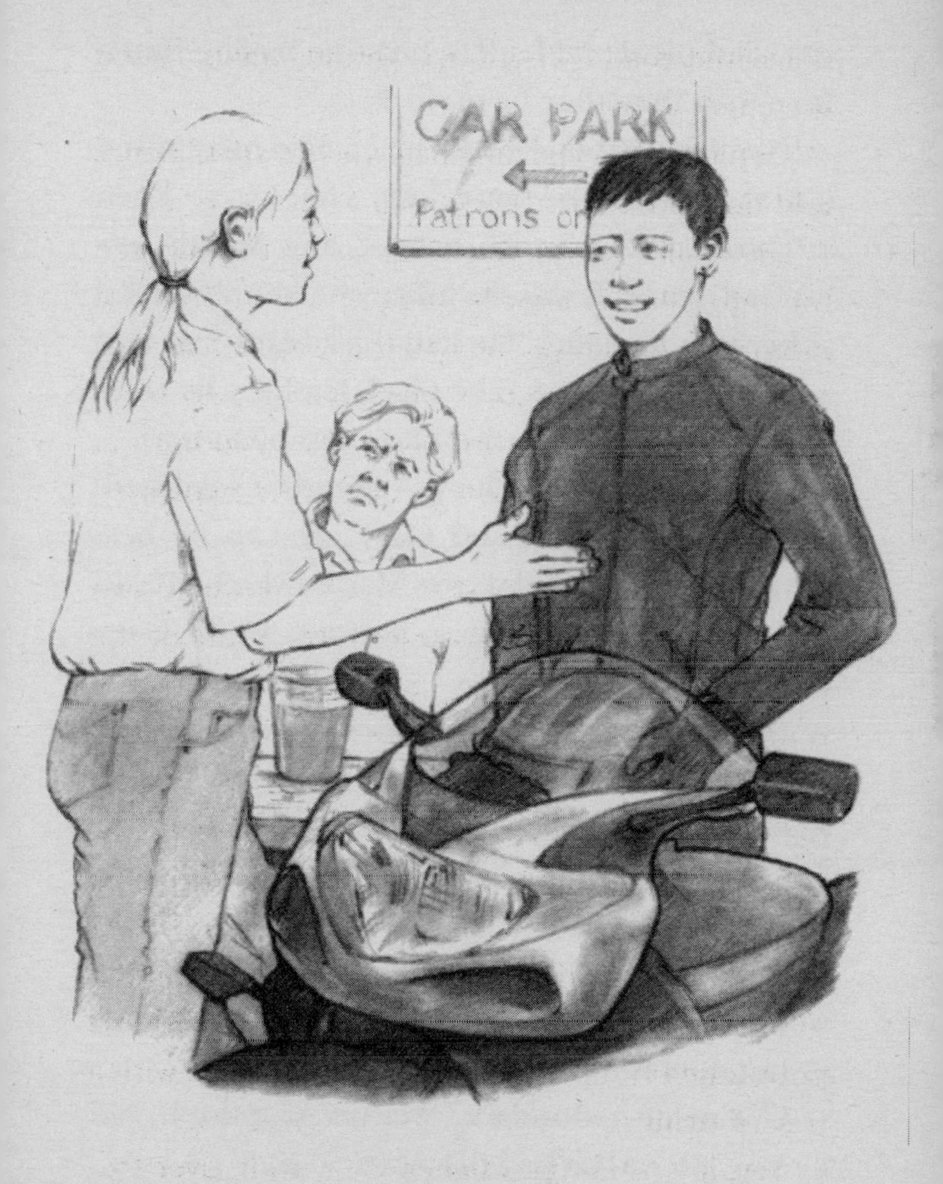
CAR PARK
Patrons

crowded picnic table. 'He must be having lunch here with the other farm workers.'

It seemed that one of the bikers had recognised him too. 'Gary?' the boy called. 'Hey, Gary!' Then he pulled off his crash helmet, and Mandy saw his face clearly. It was the biker who had shrugged at her that morning. He had thick black hair and a long, pointed face. The black leathers he wore for protection emphasised how skinny he was.

'Now I know who he is,' Mandy exclaimed. 'Martin Tucker! He and Gary used to be best friends.' She frowned. It was Martin who had held poor Snowy struggling in the air, while Gary teased her.

'He used to be a bit of a hooligan, didn't he?' James remembered. 'His family moved to Walton a couple of years ago.'

Gary got up from his lunch and walked over. 'All right, Martin?' he said, shaking hands with the skinny boy. 'I haven't seen you around for a while. I thought you were working for that garage in London as a mechanic.'

'Got made redundant.' Martin grimaced. 'No money, no way to pay the rent.'

'Bad luck, mate,' Gary sympathised.

'Anyway, I thought I'd spend some time back up here,' Martin went on. He waved to the other bikers. 'Rejoin the Walton Wranglers!'

'I see you've got some new members,' Gary noted.

Martin nodded. 'So, how are you getting on with mucking out cows, or whatever it is you do?'

'He does much more than that,' Mandy muttered indignantly to James.

Gary shrugged and smiled. 'I don't think it's going to make me a fortune, but I like it.'

'That's rough,' said Martin. 'I thought all farmers were rich!' He laughed. 'You should go on strike, Gary. Come riding with us, it would be a laugh.'

'Not right now, thanks. Maybe I'll catch up with you later,' said Gary evenly.

'Martin Tucker knows nothing,' Mandy whispered to James. 'Gary loves his job. Only people like Sam Western think farming's just about money.'

'All right then, mate,' Martin said to Gary, putting his helmet back on. 'We'll be hanging out at the usual place. See you later!'

Gary waved the lads off, then went back to his lunch. Sam Western, clearly annoyed at the interruption to his quiet drink, glared at him.

Mandy pulled a face as the noisy bikes disappeared into the distance. 'Come on,' she said to James, checking the road was clear before crossing. 'Let's fill this last bag and call it a day!'

James nodded. 'I've got to go shopping with my mum this afternoon, but we can meet up tomorrow morning and cycle to the farm park to deliver the food. I just hope Chocky appreciates it!'

Mandy spent the afternoon back at Animal Ark working on her holiday project. 'Is it supper-time soon, Mum?' she asked, wandering into the cool kitchen when she had finished. 'Collecting all those plants has given me a real appetite!'

Emily Hope eyed the two carrier bags on the kitchen floor and smiled. 'Chocky will need one too by the looks of this lot!'

'I hope she likes what we've got for her,' said Mandy. 'What are we having?'

'Cauliflower cheese,' said Mrs Hope. 'I know we had it a couple of nights ago, but–'

'That's brilliant, Mum!' Mandy cried.

Mrs Hope frowned, a lock of red hair falling over her freckled forehead. 'Is it?'

'Of course it is!' Mandy crossed the kitchen and started to gather up the discarded leaves and stalks on the kitchen worktop where her mum had been preparing the meal. 'These are the best bits of the cauliflower to give to guinea-pigs. Dad says they really love them.'

Mrs Hope rolled her eyes. 'You've gone guinea-pig crazy,' she declared with a grin.

'If you saw Chocky, you'd understand!' Mandy promised her. 'I'm going to make sure she gets the best food around, so that she's ready for her new babies.'

After supper, Mandy headed upstairs for bed. She settled back under the duvet as daylight faded from the evening sky. Closing her eyes, she looked forward to visiting Pets' Corner with James tomorrow.

Only once was she troubled in her sleep. In the dead of night, she was woken for a while by the distant sound of motorbikes speeding along the dark, deserted lanes round Welford.

Three

Mandy's alarm clock woke her at half-past six. She had set it early so she could pick some fresh plants for the guinea-pigs before meeting James at nine.

Keeping her eyes shut, Mandy groped about with one hand for the clock on her bedside table. But even when she had switched off the bell she could still hear a persistent ringing. It was the phone downstairs.

'Who's calling at this hour?' came her dad's bleary voice as he shuffled down the stairs.

Suddenly Mandy found she was wide awake.

Phone calls at odd hours in this house meant only one thing. Someone must need a vet. Worriedly, she sat up in bed, straining to hear her dad's words.

'Emily!' Adam Hope's call from downstairs sounded urgent. 'We've got a big problem.' Mandy heard her dad's footsteps thudding up the stairs. 'Get dressed, quick!'

Mandy leaped out of bed and flung her bedroom door open. 'Dad! What's happened?'

Emily Hope, her red hair tangled, was already standing on the landing. 'Who was that on the phone?'

'Mr Marsh,' said Mr Hope grimly. He dashed past her into the bedroom, unbuttoning his pyjama top. 'Reporting the worst case of vandalism he's ever seen.'

Mandy felt the knot of worry in her stomach tighten. Mr Marsh was the manager of Woodbridge Farm Park. 'Vandals?' she echoed. 'What have they done?'

'According to Mr Marsh, they've trashed the whole place,' her dad explained as he kicked off his slippers and pulled on a pair of socks. 'They've done no end of damage. They've broken down fences, smashed windows, flung paint around – and let loose a lot of the animals.'

'Oh, no,' muttered Emily Hope, instantly looking round for her clothes.

Mr Hope paused and looked solemnly at Mandy. 'Half the stock is running around scared stiff and the other half seems to be missing altogether.'

Mandy thought of all the animals in the Farm Park – Snowy, Chocky, Viking and the others. She felt her cheeks burn red with anger. 'How could anyone be so stupid?' she spluttered.

Mrs Hope pulled on an old jumper over her T-shirt. 'What about Mr and Mrs Woodbridge? Didn't they hear anything?'

Adam Hope shook his head. 'They were away last night,' he said. 'Mr Marsh is trying to get hold of them now. He's getting the police down there, too. He only realised something was wrong at the farm when he saw the Woodbridges' peacock preening himself in his back garden.'

'Dad . . .' Mandy swallowed hard. She had a question to ask but dreaded what the answer might be. 'Did Mr Marsh say anything about Pets' Corner?'

Mr Hope paused. 'No, I'm afraid he didn't.'

'Get dressed, Mandy,' Emily Hope told her. 'You'd better come with us so you can see for yourself. It sounds like we're going to need all the help we can get!'

Mandy nodded and headed back to her room, leaving her parents to finish getting ready. 'I'll call James,' she said over her shoulder. 'I'm sure he'll want to help too.'

'Good idea,' Mr Hope called after her. 'But unless he's up and about already, I'm afraid he'll have to join us down there. We've got to get going. Mr Marsh wants us there as soon as possible!'

James was far from being ready when Mandy called him. His mum answered the phone, and was shocked to hear what had happened to the Woodbridges. She brought the cordless phone to James in his room.

'It's practically the middle of the night,' James grumbled. 'What's up?'

'Everything,' Mandy told him, trying to tie her

shoelaces with one hand as she blurted out the whole story. 'Why would anyone do something so horrible?' she finished. James didn't answer, and she frowned. 'James, are you still there?'

'Sorry, I was just thinking,' he told her. 'Mandy, I was woken up in the night by the sound of motorbikes.'

'So was I,' Mandy suddenly remembered. 'Do you think Martin and his gang could have anything to do with the vandalism?' she asked breathlessly.

'Well,' James answered cautiously, 'you said that they didn't seem too bothered about frightening the sheep when they were blocking the lane, did they?'

Mandy's mind raced. She shook her head to clear it. 'I suppose we'll just have to see what the police say about it,' she said. Just then, she heard her dad calling her from outside, and the smooth starting of the Land-rover's engine. 'I've got to go.'

'I'll join you as soon as I can,' James promised. 'Bye!'

As Mandy rushed through the kitchen to the back door, she saw the two big bags of plants that she and James had spent so long picking the day before. She bit her lip. Would Chocky, Abby and the others still be at Woodbridge Farm Park to enjoy them? She decided to think positively and take the treats anyway. Grabbing the bags, she ran outside and jumped into the back of the Land-rover. As Mr Hope drove away, Mandy's heart was thumping hard. What were they going to find at the farm?

'Look out, Dad!' Mandy called, as the Land-rover turned into the track leading to the farm. But Mr Hope was already braking.

'Sally!' exclaimed Emily Hope. 'What are you doing out here?'

Sally, a large saddleback pig, was snuffling about directly in their path. As the Land-rover crawled forwards, she swung her big head round in their direction and twitched her muddy snout. Quickly losing interest in the visitors, the pig returned to digging up roots in the verge.

'Sally's shelter is in the next field, isn't it?' Mandy said.

'Not any more it isn't,' replied Mr Hope grimly.

He pointed ahead of them, and Mandy saw the wooden shelter lying smashed on its back further up the driveway.

'Seems we have a homeless pig,' observed Emily Hope. She opened the passenger door and climbed down. 'I'll check her over and make sure she doesn't get on to the main road. You go on ahead and meet Mr Marsh. I'll join you.'

'OK,' agreed Mr Hope.

The Land-rover drove on. Mandy sighed. 'I wonder what's happened to the other animals?'

Mr Hope gave her a sympathetic smile. 'I imagine you're most worried about another sort of pig,' he said quietly.

Mandy looked at her bags of weeds and nodded sadly. Then something caught her eye through the car window. 'Dad, look! The police are here!'

A police constable was standing in the churned-up mud of the field next to them, looking strangely out of place in his smart blue uniform.

'It's PC Wilde!' Mandy said, perking up a little.

'So it is!' Mr Hope pulled up beside the gateway to the field, where the broken gate hung uselessly on one hinge, and turned to Mandy. 'Can you bear to stop here for a moment while I ask him what he thinks about all this?'

Mandy nodded. She was desperate to know that Chocky was safe and well, but she was glad to see Bill Wilde had been sent here to investigate the vandalism. Mandy had first met him when the police were on the trail of badger baiters in the area. She knew he was mad about animals, and would be as keen as she was to catch the people who had wrecked the farm.

'Good morning, constable,' Mr Hope called.

PC Wilde looked up and walked over to the gate. 'Adam! And Mandy!' He smiled, but his face looked strained. 'An awful business.'

Adam Hope nodded. 'Mr Marsh sounded pretty upset. He's called us out to check the animals haven't been harmed.'

'I'm afraid you'll have to find a lot of them first,' said PC Wilde.

Mandy felt her stomach twist. 'Have you been to Pets' Corner?' she asked nervously.

'No, I haven't had a chance yet.' The policeman grimaced. 'There's enough here to keep me busy.'

'Any clues so far?' asked Mr Hope.

PC Wilde gestured to the churned-up land around them. 'Pretty plain to see,' he said.

'Tyre tracks,' Mandy said, looking at the distinctive marks in the muddy gateway.

'*Single* tyre tracks,' PC Wilde clarified. 'And Mr Marsh heard several motorbikes roaring along the roads leading from here around three-thirty this morning.'

'I heard them too, they woke me up.' Mandy

felt a cold shiver go through her. Had James been right to suspect the bikers she'd met yesterday? 'But why would they want to do this? Why would *anyone* want to do this?'

'Who can say?' PC Wilde reflected sadly. 'Well, you'd better get on. The sooner those animals are rounded up, the better. Mr and Mrs Woodbridge arrived a few minutes ago. They've gone to find Mr Marsh and check what damage has been done.'

'We'll go and find them, leave you to it,' said Adam Hope.

'See you later,' Mandy called. PC Wilde gave her a wave before crouching back down in the mud and scribbling in his notebook.

Mr and Mrs Woodbridge were talking to Mr Marsh by the entrance to the courtyard. Mrs Woodbridge smiled weakly when she saw the Land-rover pull up, and raised her pad of paper in a greeting. Mr Woodbridge simply nodded to them.

'Emily's looking after Sally,' Mr Hope told them, jumping out of the Land-rover. 'We found her at the bottom of the drive.'

'Oh, thank goodness,' cried Mrs Woodbridge,

waving a stubby pencil excitedly in the air. 'That's one more we can cross off our list.'

'List?' Mandy climbed out of the Land-rover and peered at the pad of paper the woman was holding.

'I've got a checklist of every animal in the farm,' Mrs Woodbridge explained, her mouth set in determination. 'And we won't stop until all the animals are back safe and sound.'

'Or until we've got them all accounted for, one way or another,' put in Mr Woodbridge.

'Let's hope it won't come to that,' said Adam Hope quickly. 'Now, I'd better get started.'

Mandy was scanning the list. 'Lucy and Kay, the geese . . . missing. Dilly the duck . . . missing.' Tears prickled in Mandy's eyes. 'And, oh, Dad, Viking's missing too!' She reached the end of the page and swung round to face Mrs Woodbridge. 'What about Pets' Corner?'

'There are a few places I haven't checked yet,' Mrs Woodbridge replied. 'Pets' Corner is one of them. I was just on my way there now.'

'I'll come with you,' Mandy offered, wiping her eyes with the back of her hand.

She followed Mrs Woodbridge through the courtyard. The tree stump seats and wooden tables had been overturned and strewn about. Cans of paint had been slung everywhere, and the plain barn walls and the cobbles in the yard were covered with messy splashes of white and red. But Pets' Corner was much, much worse.

Mandy stared round in horror. Hutches had been overturned, splintered and cracked where they had been trampled on. Bales of hay had been torn apart and chucked about, along with bulky rolls of chicken wire. The lamps had been ripped down from the beams, and the power leads lay in ominous black coils. Here and there, Mandy spotted guinea-pigs amid the mess; small groups cowering in corners, or bolder individuals chomping lazily on the scattered hay.

'Where's Chocky?' Mandy breathed.

'Oh, goodness,' gasped Mrs Woodbridge. 'Her hutch has been knocked right over.'

Mandy walked forward unsteadily, feeling like her legs had turned to jelly. She didn't want to look too closely at the hutch, for fear of what she might see. The door to the sleeping quarters had come unlatched and it had fallen open like a drawbridge. Mandy heard a soft peeping noise from underneath it, and her heart skittered with joy.

Mrs Woodbridge bent down and scooped up a small dark shape in both hands. 'It's Abby!' she whispered happily, looking closely at the trembling guinea-pig. 'Scared half to death, but apart from that she seems all right.'

'Thank goodness,' Mandy whispered back. 'But where's Chocky?'

'Can you lift up one of the hutches, Mandy?' asked Mrs Woodbridge, straightening up and beginning to sound calmer. 'We can gather up the little ones and make a proper record of who we're missing.'

While Mrs Woodbridge continued to smooth Abby's glossy dark coat, Mandy hauled one of the larger hutches back on to the breezeblocks that had supported it. She scooped up handfuls of sawdust and straw to make the floor comfortable, and Abby became the first occupant.

'That's great,' Mrs Woodbridge told her. 'We'll use this one for the girls, but we'll need a separate place to house the boys.' She pointed to another large hutch, lying on the ground with its lid pulled off. 'This one will do,' she said, grabbing hold of one end. 'Ready? Heave!'

They soon had the second hutch the right way up, and lined with sawdust ready for the male guinea-pigs. Mandy was pleased to see that the water bottle was still intact, and nearly full, so the guinea-pigs would have something to drink.

Together, Mandy and Mrs Woodbridge hunted all over the barn for the missing animals, sifting through piles of hay and carefully lifting aside pieces of splintered wood. But all the while, Mandy's mind was racing. If Abby had stayed close by her hutch, why wasn't Chocky there too? She hoped against hope that the pregnant guinea-pig would be found safe and sound. But the more they searched unsuccessfully, the lower Mandy's spirits sank.

'She's gone,' Mandy told herself quietly and with horrible certainty. 'Chocky's gone.'

Four

'I think we have to face facts, Mandy,' said Mrs Woodbridge at last. 'We've searched this barn from top to bottom, and we're still missing two rabbits and three guinea-pigs.'

'More than three guinea-pigs, if you count Chocky's babies,' Mandy pointed out. She tried to swallow the hard lump in her throat. There was no time to cry. 'The missing animals must've run away through the barn door,' she added. 'Why didn't they stay here where it's safe?'

'They would have been very frightened,' said Mrs Woodbridge gravely.

'But guinea-pigs and rabbits are only little, they can't have got too far,' Mandy went on determinedly. 'Even if they've got a six-hour head start on us. We'll just have to look everywhere, all over the village if we have to, until we've found them all.'

'That's the spirit, Mandy,' smiled Mrs Woodbridge. 'I suppose we should be grateful it's not a lot worse,' she added with forced brightness. 'At least none of the small animals has been badly hurt so far.'

'They were lucky,' Mandy agreed. Aside from some cuts and scratches, she and Mrs Woodbridge had found no serious injuries. 'Even so, Mum and Dad should still give them all a proper check-up.'

'We certainly will,' came her mother's voice from the barn doorway. 'But I think you'll have to help us with that, Mandy. We've really got our work cut out here.'

'OK, Mum,' Mandy said. 'But Chocky's gone, and lots of the others are missing too. I really need to start looking for them as soon as possible.'

Emily Hope gave her daughter a hug. 'I know, love.' She smiled warmly. 'If it's any consolation, Sally's back safely. I left her a trail of windfall apples to follow back to the farm, and Mr Woodbridge was able to shoo her into a pen.'

'Well done!' Mandy said, smiling back.

'What about the other animals?' asked Mrs Woodbridge. The look on her face suggested she was bracing herself for the worst.

'Well, the Ayrshires are all safe and sound in their cowshed,' Emily Hope began positively. 'Dilly the duck's still missing, and Adam's just cleaning up one of the others. Her feathers have been covered in paint. Hopefully, she hasn't swallowed enough for it to be harmful.' She sighed. 'I'm afraid a lot of paint tins were thrown into the chicken coop. One of the hens has hurt her wing. I want to look at her next, as it may be broken.'

Mandy shook her head sadly.

'On a brighter note, Molly and Mr Woodbridge are rounding up the sheep that were let out in the lower field,' Mrs Hope went on. 'They're all accounted for, with no signs of injury.'

Mandy was glad to hear that Snowy and her lambs were safe and well. 'Any sign of Viking yet?' she asked.

'I'm afraid not,' her mum admitted. 'Nor the pot-bellied pigs. It looks like we're going to have a bit of a hunt on our hands for them.'

'But Mum, what if some of the animals have got on to the roads? What if they've been hit by a car!'

'It's still early in the morning, Mandy,' Mrs Hope said soothingly. 'There won't have been much traffic on the roads, so they should be all right.'

'Oh, if only I'd been here when it happened,' sighed Mrs Woodbridge, wringing her hands.

Emily Hope placed her hand gently on the older woman's shoulder. 'None of this is your fault,' she assured her. 'We'll get it all sorted out, don't you worry.'

'Thanks, Emily,' smiled Mrs Woodbridge. 'Yes, if we all pull together, I suppose . . .' A thought seemed to strike her. 'You know, Gary's not turned up for work yet. He was due in at six, where can he be?'

'I'm sure he'll be here soon,' said Mrs Hope. 'It's such a shame Simon's away on holiday,' she sighed. 'He'd be glad to come up and help.'

Mandy nodded. Simon was the practice nurse at Animal Ark and a good friend. He was efficient, gentle and sure-handed with animals.

'Well, I'd better let you get on,' said Mrs Woodbridge. 'There's so much still to do.'

Emily Hope surveyed the mess in the barn and nodded thoughtfully. 'Starting with these guinea-pigs.'

'You said I could help, Mum,' Mandy reminded her. 'None of them is badly hurt, but there are some scratches to clean up.'

'OK, Mandy, I'll leave you to it,' said Mrs Hope. 'Can you fetch some clean towels, please, Mrs Woodbridge? Wrapping a guinea-pig up in one will stop it becoming stressed during the examination, and make it easier to control. Then you can clean the cuts with some warm salty water, Mandy. Oh, and Mrs Woodbridge, I suppose it's too much to hope you've got some lavender oil in the house too?'

Mrs Woodbridge nodded excitedly. 'As a matter of fact, I do.'

'Well, once the wounds are clean, you can dress them with a little lavender,' explained Emily Hope. 'It'll act like an antiseptic and won't hurt the animal if it's licked off.'

'Great,' said Mrs Woodbridge. 'Mandy, I'll be right back.'

As she bustled out of the barn, Mandy turned to her mum. 'Can I borrow the mobile?' she asked. 'I think I'll phone Gran and Grandad, they always get up early. Maybe they could go out looking for some of the other animals, or call around to see if anyone's spotted them.'

'Good idea,' said Emily Hope, handing over the phone. 'Well, I'd better get back to the front line.'

'It's such a shame that Gary's not here to help,' Mandy said.

Mrs Hope shrugged. 'Perhaps he's sick.'

'He was fine yesterday lunchtime. James and I saw him . . .' Mandy tailed off before she could finish her sentence, but it seemed to echo on in her head – *we saw him talking to those bikers*. She pushed the thought away, and told herself she was being silly. Gary couldn't be involved with any of this. He loved the animals too much.

'Good luck, Mandy.' Emily Hope jogged away, dodging round a fallen hay bale on her way out of the barn. 'If there's anything you're not sure how to treat, come and find me,' she said.

'I will,' Mandy promised. 'See you later.'

In the quiet of the empty barn, Mandy's thoughts turned again to Chocky. While she knew that the other animals needed treatment as soon as possible, part of her wanted to go straight outside to search the whole farm for the pregnant guinea-pig. Mandy couldn't help imagining how Chocky would have tumbled about when the hutch was knocked over, and how scared she must have been in the darkness.

'At least she wasn't so badly hurt she couldn't run away,' Mandy reasoned to herself. 'Chocky has probably found somewhere safe and quiet to hide. I'm sure she's all right, wherever she is. She *has* to be.'

A chorus of friendly chirrups from the guinea-pigs and rabbits around her started up, as if trying to reassure her. Mandy smiled, and started dialling her grandad's number into the mobile phone.

'Oh, no,' came a horrified voice from behind her before she could make the call. 'I thought the rest was bad, but look at the state of this place!'

Mandy spun round to see Dillon standing in the doorway. He was red-faced and panting.

'Chocky's gone,' she told him shakily. 'She's run away.'

Dillon's face fell still further as he walked over to join Mandy in the middle of the wreckage. 'Who else is missing?'

'See for yourself.' Mandy showed him the list Mrs Woodbridge had made of the absent animals from all over the farm. 'As soon as I've patched up these pigs, I'm going to start hunting round.'

'We could go together,' offered Dillon. 'I've been looking after them all summer, so I know what they all look like.'

'Hi, Dillon. You don't know where your brother's got to, do you?' said another voice. Mrs Woodbridge appeared in the doorway.

Dillon frowned. 'You mean he's not here?'

'I only wish he were,' she went on. 'This is the worst day he could've chosen to oversleep.'

'He . . . I mean . . .' Dillon seemed flustered for a moment, then he stopped altogether.

Mrs Woodbridge didn't press him for an explanation. She just shook her head and collected the animal checklist from Dillon. Then she turned to Mandy. 'Here's the towel and the lavender oil your mum asked for. If you're sure you can manage here, I think I'd better finish my round-up of the animals.'

Mandy nodded, and Mrs Woodbridge hurried away.

'Come on, Dillon,' Mandy said quietly, noticing her friend's glum expression. 'She isn't cross with you.'

'I know,' said Dillon. 'It's just what she said about Gary . . .' He tailed off.

'Is anything wrong?' Mandy asked gently.

Dillon looked as if he wanted to tell her something, then he blushed and fell silent, shaking his head.

Mandy frowned, but she knew she couldn't force Dillon to talk. Besides, there was work to be done. 'Look, Dillon,' she said, changing the subject and beckoning him over to the back of the barn. 'We've set up some temporary guinea-pig shelters. Come and help me decide who needs treating first.'

They began with Starsky, a rex guinea-pig with the characteristic frizzy short-haired coat. He had cut his ear, probably on a sharp piece of chicken wire. Dillon held the towel and, carefully, Mandy wrapped Starsky up in it. The guinea-pig worked his two front paws loose from the folds of the towel and managed to wriggle free. Mandy wrapped him up again, this time making sure his legs were well tucked in.

'He looks like a baby in a blanket!' remarked Dillon, holding him still while Mandy gently rubbed a wet cotton-wool swab over his cut ear.

Starsky seemed to understand they were trying to help him, and by the time Mandy dabbed the lavender oil on the cleaned-up cut, he was purring quietly.

'Shall I do the next one?' Dillon offered.

'OK,' said Mandy. 'They're more used to you than me, anyway.' She felt for the phone in her pocket. 'And while you're doing that, I'm going to ring Gran and Grandad.'

Mandy went outside and walked along the

hedge-lined path that led to Viking's empty paddock, keeping an eye out for Chocky or any of the other stray animals.

It wasn't a guinea-pig that greeted her as she got nearer the field, but two ducks wandering along the track in the same direction. One of them had a swagger in its step that Mandy recognised at once. She had kept a diary of the duck's activities for a school project a couple of years ago.

'Dilly!' Mandy breathed.

The duck turned round as Mandy approached. Then she quickened her pace along the path, as if suddenly afraid. The other duck waddled after Dilly with an anxious quack.

Mandy crept softly after both of them. 'Don't be scared,' she murmured. 'I only want to take you back to the pond.' She considered trying to get past the ducks and shooing them back the way they had come, but the path was too narrow here. But if the ducks reached the stile at the end before she did, they could escape into the open field, and catching them would be a lot harder. She had to get there ahead of them.

'Oh, dear,' came a woman's voice from somewhere on the other side of the hedge. 'Is there anybody about? Hello? Oh, heavens.'

Mandy thought she recognised the worried voice coming from Viking's paddock. She straightened up and began to walk faster.

Quacking noisily, the ducks rushed forward. Mandy couldn't get ahead of them in time. The ducks flapped underneath the stile at the end of the path and into the field. As Mandy clambered over behind them, she heard the anxious voice again: 'Keep away, please!'

Realising the ducks would have to wait for a moment, Mandy crossed to the fence of Viking's field. The wooden posts had been uprooted, and the wire mesh between them stamped down almost flat into the ground.

In the middle of the next field stood Lydia Fawcett, the owner of High Cross Farm. Beside her was a big bundle of wire netting. Lydia was holding herself as still as a statue. With a jolt, Mandy saw why.

The great grey shape of Apollo, the Clydesdale stallion, loomed over Lydia Fawcett with his nostrils flared and his sides heaving. Apollo normally lived in the next field but one. As Mandy watched, he threw back his head and neighed loudly.

'What's happening?' Mandy called.

'Mandy!' Lydia Fawcett called back, her voice high-pitched with concern. 'This horse came running up from nowhere . . . and he's hurt himself.'

Mandy's stomach clenched as she noticed a streak of blood down one of the stallion's front legs.

'I'm a bit nervous around large horses,' Lydia went on, keeping her eyes glued on Apollo.

Apollo let out another neigh, and snorted menacingly through his nose.

'Don't worry,' Mandy said. 'I've met Apollo before, perhaps he'll recognise me.' She began to walk slowly towards him, reaching out with one hand. The horse swung his head round to look at her as she approached. Then he wheeled away and galloped off, his massive hooves thudding heavily on the turf.

Mandy stood still and breathed deeply to keep

herself calm. 'Apollo!' she called firmly. 'Steady, boy.'

But Apollo tossed his head and skittered off to the far corner of the field. He stopped dead with his head held high and the whites of his eyes showing in alarm.

'Careful, Mandy!' warned Lydia Fawcett. 'Don't go too near.'

'My mum and dad are with the Woodbridges,' Mandy called over her shoulder. 'Can you fetch them? I'll stay here with Apollo.'

'OK,' said Miss Fawcett as she hurried away. 'I'll be right back!'

Mandy walked over to Apollo. 'You've hurt your leg,' she said, keeping her voice low and steady. 'Stay nice and still, and Lydia will get help for you.'

Apollo looked down at her for a few moments as if considering her words. Then he flattened his ears back against his head and snaked his neck towards her with his teeth bared. It looked as if he was going to bite her!

Five

'Don't you dare!' Mandy ordered. Her body was shaking, but her voice rang out with authority.

Apollo stopped, and took a pace back.

'I should hope so!' Mandy went on in the same clear tone. She took a step forward. She knew she had to stay close to his side so he wouldn't be able to kick out at her. 'Just because Viking's gone for a walkabout, it doesn't mean you can move into his field.'

She kept up a steady stream of conversation, not trying to reach out to the stallion, but standing quietly beside him. After a while, the Clydesdale seemed a lot calmer. His breathing became deeper and more regular, and he let Mandy stroke his sweating neck. 'Good boy,' she told him. 'That's better, isn't it?' She looked down at the wound on his leg. 'Don't you worry, we'll soon get that looked at.' She glanced round anxiously, firstly for the escaped ducks, then for any sign of Lydia Fawcett returning with her mum and dad.

Just then the roar of a car engine disturbed the silence. Over the top of the dry stone wall, Mandy watched as a white van pulled up beside her. Apollo shifted restlessly, but Mandy laid her hand on his shoulder to soothe him.

She watched in surprise as Ernie Bell clambered out of the battered van. What was going on? First Lydia Fawcett had turned up from nowhere, and now Ernie Bell.

'Hello, Ernie,' Mandy called.

'Where's Lydia?' Ernie Bell demanded. 'She was supposed to be meeting me here to help fix the damage to the fence. Stuart Woodbridge called her first thing this morning, then she called me.'

Mandy couldn't help smiling. Ernie Bell was

well known for being grumpy and bad-tempered. But she knew that he was a lot milder underneath it all, with a soft spot for Lydia Fawcett in particular. Now, thanks to Ernie and Lydia's kindness, the Woodbridges would soon have their paddock repaired.

With a jump, Ernie noticed the stallion towering over Mandy. 'This old fellow got loose, did he? Just like those geese!'

'Lucy and Kay?' Mandy asked quickly. 'Have you seen them?'

'Seen them?' Ernie echoed. 'I've got them in the back of my van!'

'But that's *brilliant*!' Mandy could have shouted with joy, but she didn't want to upset Apollo again.

'They were making a terrible noise outside the Fox and Goose,' Ernie went on. 'I thought I'd better pick them up, since I was coming here anyway.'

'Lydia's roll of fencing wire is over there,' Mandy told him, pointing to the bundle in the centre of the field. 'But be careful, it's sharp. I think Apollo has cut himself on it.'

Ernie waved aside her concern as he marched

off to the stile in the roadside wall that enabled ramblers to get into the field. 'Hang about,' he said. 'There's a couple of ducks coming this way!'

'Don't let them get out of the field, Mr Bell!' Mandy urged him. 'They need to be taken back to the pond.'

'Ducks, geese, goats,' grumbled Ernie Bell as he shooed the ducks ahead of him. 'Whatever next?'

Mandy had to hide her smile. Just then, she heard a call from behind her.

It was Lydia, standing timidly at the far end of the field, clearly not wanting to get too close to Apollo again. But standing right behind her was Adam Hope, holding his first-aid box and a head collar.

Mandy waved enthusiastically as her dad came over to join her.

'Well done, Mandy,' Mr Hope told her with a smile. He buckled the head collar on to Apollo and peered down at the horse's leg. 'Looks like this chap's got a nasty scratch. Still, it won't take long to clean him up.'

'How's the duck with paint on her feathers?' Mandy asked him.

'She'll be fine,' Mr Hope assured her. 'I've got the worst of it off. And your mum is looking after the hen. Luckily her wing's not broken.'

There was a loud honk from the back of Mr Bell's van and Adam Hope looked up in surprise.

Mandy laughed. 'It's Lucy and Kay, the geese!' she explained. She gasped as she suddenly remembered something. 'Oh no! I forgot to call Grandad!'

'Why not call him on your way back to Pets' Corner?' her dad suggested. 'We've had another couple of visitors that I think you'll be glad to see!'

Mandy left Apollo with her dad and jogged back to the Pets' Corner courtyard, dialling as she ran. Soon she was telling Grandad Hope what had happened, feeling a fresh wave of dismay as she reached Pets' Corner and looked around her at the damage.

'So it's all hands to the pump, is it?' her grandad said kindly. 'Well, we'll get busy putting search parties together round the village. With your gran organising things, we'll have those animals rounded up in no time!'

Mandy managed to smile. 'I hope so,' she said. Then she saw a familiar figure enter the courtyard – James had arrived on his bike. He was flushed and his hair was plastered to his forehead.

'I've got to go, Grandad,' Mandy said. 'Good luck, see you later!'

'There you are!' puffed James. In his bike basket was a thick paper grocery bag full of the plants he'd picked yesterday.

'Thanks for coming,' Mandy called. 'But Dad said there were *two* visitors waiting for me. Is Gary with you?'

'No.' James looked puzzled. 'Isn't he already here?'

Mandy shook her head.

'Well,' said James, reaching into the bag of weeds with both hands, 'perhaps your dad meant *this* little visitor!' He carefully lifted out a sandy-coloured rabbit, its long ears flopping, chewing happily on a plant stem.

'Dillon, quick!' Mandy called into the barn. 'James has found one of the missing rabbits!'

Dillon was out in seconds. 'Dandelion!' he whooped, taking the rabbit from James's outstretched hands. 'Well done, James, that's brilliant. Where did you find her?'

'Halfway up the hill,' said James.

'She got all that way?' Mandy was incredulous.

'Afraid so,' James reported. 'I stopped for a breather by the side of the road, and saw her hopping along the grassy verge. I thought I'd better grab her, quick.'

'That means the only rabbit still missing is Springer,' said Dillon.

Mandy beamed at her friends, suddenly feeling hopeful again. 'If we can find one, we can find them all!' she declared.

Dillon nodded enthusiastically. 'I've checked over the guinea-pigs' injuries and done all I can,' he said. 'So we can get on with some serious searching right away.'

'Room for two more?' came a cheery voice. It was PC Wilde, holding his helmet out in front of him. Mr Marsh was walking alongside him, looking tired, but smiling.

'Who have you found?' Mandy asked breathlessly.

She and Dillon ran over to greet them, James catching them up once he'd parked his bike.

'A pair of guinea-pigs,' announced Mr Marsh.

PC Wilde held out his helmet for Mandy, James and Dillon to see. 'I was looking at the tyre tracks in that field, and found them sitting in one of the ruts!'

A long-haired chocolate and cream coloured guinea-pig nestled in the policeman's helmet, peering up at them through the fringe that hung over its eyes. Nuzzled up beside it was another guinea-pig that reminded Mandy of a Siamese kitten. Its fur was a beautiful grey-white with dark pointing at the ears, nose and feet.

'Frisker and Twitch!' Dillon exclaimed, smiling at the guinea-pigs.

'Well, I'd be grateful if you could take them out of police custody,' joked PC Wilde. 'I've eliminated them from my inquiries!'

Dillon scooped up the long-haired bundle from the policeman's helmet and handed it to Mandy. 'Frisker's a Peruvian,' he told her. He passed the smaller guinea-pig to James, who carefully held it to his chest. 'And Twitch is a Himalayan crested.'

'You know a lot about animals, Dillon,' PC Wilde observed. 'Runs in the family, does it?'

Dillon looked puzzled.

'Well, Mr Marsh tells me your brother works here.' PC Wilde brushed out the inside of his helmet before placing it back on his head. 'Gary Lewis?'

Mr Marsh nodded. 'Yes, where is your brother today? He should have started work two hours ago.'

Dillon looked down at his feet. 'I'm not really sure where he is, Mr Marsh.'

'Had a late night last night, did he?' PC Wilde inquired.

'I don't know,' Dillon mumbled. 'Maybe.'

Mandy looked at him with concern, remembering how he'd suddenly gone quiet before, in the barn. She was convinced there was something Dillon wasn't telling them about his brother.

'Well, if you see him back home later, Dillon,' Mr Marsh went on, watching him carefully, 'tell him we were asking after him, all right?'

Dillon nodded without looking up. 'OK.'

'Come on. Let's put these guinea-pigs back in the shelter,' Mandy suggested, leading the way back inside the barn.

Dillon watched in silence as James and Mandy gently placed the guinea-pigs in the boys' hutch.

'Just Chocky and Springer still to find,' Mandy said with relief. James grinned, but Dillon said nothing.

Mandy looked at her friend. 'You were going to

tell me something earlier, Dillon,' she gently prompted him.

Dillon took a deep breath. 'Gary didn't come home last night. His bed's not been slept in. I thought I'd find him here. Instead, there's all this mess . . .' Dillon shrugged helplessly. 'Maybe we should start looking for Gary as well. A missing person on top of our missing animals.'

Mandy tried to give him a reassuring smile. 'Don't worry, Dillon. He probably just stayed over with a friend or something, and overslept . . .' But even as she said the words, Mandy remembered watching Gary talk to Martin and the other bikers outside the pub. He'd said that he might see them later. Had he gone for the promised ride with the gang after all, and ended up here?

For a second she pictured the Gary Lewis from a few years back, taunting poor Snowy. Then she shook her head. It just didn't make sense that Gary would do any of this. He loved animals, and loved his job here too . . .'

Mandy's head was a whirl of conflicting thoughts. On the one hand she wanted to find someone to blame for causing this terrible mess, and for hurting the animals. On the other, she didn't want Dillon's own brother to be one of the culprits. From the worried look on his face, she realised that some of these thoughts must be bothering Dillon as well.

'Come on, Dillon,' Mandy said. 'Let's go and have one last look round the courtyard for Chocky, just in case.'

Back outside in the sunshine, Mandy noticed that PC Wilde and Mr Marsh were looking at something on one of the paint-splattered barns.

'Look at this big smear, here,' said PC Wilde. 'One of the intruders must've leaned against the wall.'

Mr Marsh nodded gravely. 'That'll have made a right mess of their clothes.'

'And it might help us to find who did it,' said PC Wilde.

'But we know who did it,' retorted Mr Marsh. 'Those bikers. Who else could it be?'

'All the evidence so far is circumstantial,' PC Wilde pointed out. 'All we can prove is that some people drove through the upper field on motorbikes. I can question the Walton Wranglers, but even if they did do it, without more evidence we won't be able to bring charges.'

Mr Marsh's face cleared in understanding. 'So if one of them had white paint smeared over their clothes, it would be hard to deny they were here when the vandalism was done?'

'Precisely,' said PC Wilde. 'Now, let's go and look at the hen-coop again. I want to look at those paint tins.' The two men walked out of the courtyard.

'I wish I knew where the vandals were right now,' muttered James, clenching his fists into tight balls.

'I'd settle for knowing where Chocky is,' Mandy said. She started peering under the overturned picnic tables while James went off to check behind the barns. Then they both looked into the barn that was home to the Ayrshire cows, full of their strong animal smell. The cows lowed as Mandy and James approached, watching them curiously with huge dark eyes as they checked the straw-scattered ground. But there was no sign of Chocky.

With a helpless shrug, Mandy and James left

the cows and returned to Dillon in the courtyard.

'It looks like we'll have to look further afield,' said James.

Dillon nodded. 'The road leading from here down to the village could be our best bet.'

'Look, there's Dad,' said Mandy. She waved as Adam Hope appeared with his first-aid kit from the direction of Viking's field. 'Let's find out how Apollo is, and tell him we're going on a guinea-pig hunt.'

Mr Hope told them that the injured stallion was doing fine, and waiting in Viking's paddock for Mr Woodbridge to take him back down to the lower field. Meanwhile, Ernie Bell was making good progress on securing the fence. 'All we need now is a goat to put in it!' Mr Hope concluded.

'Hopefully, Gran and Grandad's search party will find Viking soon,' Mandy said.

Her dad grinned. 'No doubt they've got half of Welford out looking!'

Mandy laughed, and looked at James and Dillon. 'Well, we'll keep an eye out for him as well. We're going to go searching for Springer and poor Chocky, right down into the village if we have to.

It's a good job the sun is shining, as we might be out for the rest of the day!'

Mr Hope frowned. 'Actually, Mandy, that's not such good news,' he said quietly. 'We don't want it to get any hotter. Guinea-pigs can suffer badly from heat exhaustion, and pregnant ones are especially vulnerable.'

Mandy looked up at him, suddenly fearful. 'What might happen to her, Dad? Tell me.'

'I don't like to say this,' Adam Hope said seriously, 'but unless Chocky is brought inside and cooled right down, she and her babies are in great danger.'

Six

Mandy clenched her fists in determination. 'We *will* find Chocky,' she promised. 'But how will we know if she has got heat exhaustion?'

'Well,' said Mr Hope, considering. 'She won't be able to stand up, and her breathing rate will be very fast.'

Mandy thought back to the way she had swaddled up the injured guinea-pig in the barn. 'Would it help if we wrapped her in a wet towel?'

'That would be perfect,' said Adam Hope. 'But

you must be careful not to leave her in it for too long, or you could chill her.'

James nodded. 'And maybe we should take along some water for her to drink? That would help to cool her down.'

Mr Hope shook his head. 'Whatever you do, don't let her drink anything straight away. Guinea-pigs aren't good at swallowing at the best of times, and the water could get into Chocky's lungs. Wait till she's breathing normally, then give her something to drink.'

'We could take one of the animal water bottles from Pets' Corner,' suggested Dillon. 'They release water in small sips, which will be easy for Chocky to swallow.'

'Good idea,' said Mandy. 'Thanks, Dad.'

'Good luck,' smiled Mr Hope. 'See you later!'

Mandy fetched a towel and a drip-feed water bottle from Pets' Corner. As an afterthought, she took a handful of dried rabbit food and put it in her pocket.

'Let's follow the main track out of the farm,' suggested James. 'Maybe some of the other animals went that way, if PC Wilde found

Frisker and Twitch in the field beside it.'

'So what are we waiting for?' said Dillon, jogging across the courtyard to fetch his bike.

'If only I had my bike,' Mandy sighed.

'Dillon and I could go on ahead,' suggested James. 'We'll cover more ground that way, while you can do some close detective work on foot!'

'I suppose so,' said Mandy. But when she reached the car park, there was a surprise waiting for her. Mandy's grandparents had just arrived, and were climbing out of their shiny camper-van. 'Gran! Grandad!' she exclaimed. 'Do you know if any of the animals have been found in the village yet?'

Gran nodded. 'The pot-bellied pigs found their way into the Post Office kitchen!' she said with a grin. 'They seemed happy enough in Mrs McFarlane's larder. When she couldn't get hold of your mum and dad, she tried Mr Gill from Greystones, the pig farm. He's going to bring them back here.'

'That's brilliant news,' Mandy beamed. 'That just leaves Viking, Springer and Chocky still to find!' Her delighted grin grew larger when she saw what they'd brought with them in the back of the van. 'My bike!' she cried. 'How did you know I'd want it?'

Grandma Hope smiled at her. 'We thought this was going to be a busy day for everyone, and we knew that you got a lift this morning with your mum and dad. So we reckoned you might like to be able to come and go as you pleased!'

Grandad lifted the bike out of the camper-van. 'Did we guess right?' he puffed.

'You guessed brilliantly!' Mandy got on her bike and grinned at James and Dillon. 'Now we're fully mobile!'

'We're going to set up a temporary café,' said Grandad Hope. 'We've organised a lot of people to come here and help clean things up. As usual, your gran's made enough sandwiches and thermoses of tea to feed a whole army of helpers.'

Grandma tutted and removed a large cake tin from the back of the van. 'Be that as it may, I'm sure it'll all be gone by this evening, especially if you have anything to do with it, Tom Hope!'

Mandy waved goodbye to her grandparents as

they carried their provisions round to the courtyard. Then she got on her bike and, together with James and Dillon, cycled slowly down the dirt track. They looked carefully to either side as they went.

'It's a shame guinea-pigs and rabbits don't leave much in the way of tracks,' sighed James. 'Welford's a big place when you're small enough to hide just about anywhere.'

'At least it's nice and quiet,' Dillon pointed out. 'You never know, we might hear them squealing.'

But a few moments later it was their brakes that were squealing as they rounded the corner and found their way was blocked.

'Gary!' breathed Dillon.

Gary Lewis was sitting in his van in the middle of the drive, talking through the open side window to Mr Woodbridge. From the pile of splintered wood on the verge, Mandy guessed the farmer had been clearing away the wreckage of Sally the pig's shelter.

'How bad is the damage?' Gary was asking.

'Very bad,' said Mr Woodbridge gravely. 'And why are you so late today?'

'I'm really sorry,' Gary said sheepishly. 'My watch alarm didn't go off. I spent all night in a tree, watching owls up on Black Tor.'

Mr Woodbridge looked at him closely. 'So you didn't see any of your motorcycling friends?'

Gary shook his head. 'Didn't hear any of them either, up there. I thought while the nights are still mild I'd get some birdwatching in.'

Mr Woodbridge fell silent, his face thoughtful. Mandy could tell that he was considering Gary's report.

Next to Mandy, Dillon breathed a long sigh of relief. 'So *that's* where Gary was.'

'Do you believe him?' asked James.

Dillon looked at him angrily. 'Don't you?'

James held up his hands in apology. 'Sorry, Dillon. I didn't mean it to come out like that.'

'I believe him,' Mandy said quietly. 'I just know Gary wouldn't get involved with something as nasty as this.'

It seemed that Mr Woodbridge agreed with her. He smiled and nodded at Gary. 'All right, lad. Hurry yourself down to the farm and pitch in with the others.'

Gary leaned out of the open car window to wave at his brother, and smiled in greeting to Mandy and James. Then he looked down and noticed the debris lying at Mr Woodbridge's feet. 'Shall I chuck this lot in the back of the van? Maybe I can fix the shelter.'

Mr Woodbridge nodded. 'If you can't, give Ernie Bell a shout. He's up in Viking's paddock.'

Gary got out and hefted the planks of wood into the back of the van. Mandy was about to lead the way on her bike when she heard a new sound. A noisy mechanical spluttering roar, rolling around the landscape, getting louder.

'It's not the bikers coming back, is it?' Mandy asked nervously.

James frowned. 'I don't think so. It sounds more like a car engine.'

'And not a very healthy one,' Dillon added.

At that moment the source of the noise became clear. A silver-blue Land-rover rounded the corner and came to an abrupt stop behind Gary's van. The engine rattled ominously, but it was drowned out by a blast on the Land-rover's horn.

Mr Woodbridge rolled his eyes up to heaven. 'That's all I need,' he muttered. 'A visit from Sam Western!'

Mr Western stuck his head indignantly out of the driver's window. 'What kind of a place is this to park?' he demanded, gesturing at Gary's van.

'What brings you here, Sam?' asked Mr Woodbridge.

'I've come from the village, and heard half your

animals are running about Welford,' Sam Western told him. 'Pigs in the post office, goats all over the place . . .'

'Goats!' cried Mandy. 'Are you talking about Viking?'

Sam Western glared at her. 'Call the thing what you want,' he grumbled. 'Some shaggy curly-horned creature was seen trotting towards Bleakfell Hall, that's all I know.'

Mandy flashed an excited smile at James and Dillon. They had a clue to where one of the missing animals might be!

'Anyway,' Sam Western went on, 'I just wanted to check you've got the situation under control.'

'Well, that's kind of you to ask, Sam,' said Mr Woodbridge, sounding surprised.

'Kind's got nothing to do with it,' said Sam Western flatly. 'I don't want to find myself having to deal with any of your strays making a mess of my land!'

Mr Woodbridge nodded wearily. 'Don't worry, I think we're getting on top of it now.' He smiled at Mandy, James and Dillon. 'I've got some very good search parties.'

'Heard it was vandals that did the damage,' Mr Western said gruffly. 'Anyone caught yet?'

'The police are still looking into the matter,' said Mr Woodbridge.

Sam Western let his gaze fall on Gary, and gave a loud sniff. 'Seems to me the prime suspect's right in front of you.'

Mandy glanced worriedly at Dillon. His cheeks were burning crimson, and he was gripping his handlebars so tightly his knuckles had turned white.

'What's that supposed to mean?' asked Mr Woodbridge stiffly.

Sam Western shrugged. 'Just that I saw this one talking with those hooligans on motorbikes yesterday lunchtime.'

Mr Woodbridge seemed to have been left speechless, and so Sam Western looked back to Gary. 'Yes, you two were always trouble when you were growing up.' He turned back to Mr Woodbridge. 'A leopard doesn't change its spots, Stuart.'

Gary opened his mouth to protest, but Mr Woodbridge held a hand up to stop him. 'Yes, well, thank you for dropping by, Sam,' he said. 'But in future I'd thank you to keep your opinions to yourself.'

'Suit yourself,' said Mr Western, winding up the window and reversing noisily back down the drive.

'He can't get away with talking to Gary like that!' protested Dillon.

'Just ignore him,' James advised. 'He's full of hot air.'

'And Mr Woodbridge doesn't believe him anyway,' Mandy added. She looked hopefully at the farmer. 'Do you?'

Mr Woodbridge scratched his head. 'No. And I like to think I'm a good judge of character,' he said to Gary. 'You've done a good job here for the last three years, that's for sure.'

'Thanks,' said Gary gratefully. 'But if Mr Western's been spouting off down the village, what will everyone else think?'

'We'll tell them he's a liar!' said Dillon hotly.

'You'll do no such thing,' said Gary. 'That'll only make things worse.'

'Sensible lad,' said Mr Woodbridge approvingly. 'Look, Gary, it might be better if you kept a low profile today. Tell PC Wilde where you were last night, then go home.'

'But I want to help,' Gary insisted.

'Well, maybe you can fetch some materials from Walton,' suggested Mr Woodbridge. 'The hen houses need fixing up, and there's a lot of redecorating to be done before we can re-open.'

'OK,' said Gary. 'As long as I'm doing something useful.'

'Come on,' Mandy said to James and Dillon. 'We've got to keep searching!'

Leaving Gary and Mr Woodbridge to their discussion, they cycled along the drive to the main road.

Soon they were rolling slowly downhill, looking about for Chocky or Springer. But there was no sign of either animal. The weather was growing steadily hotter, and Mandy's thoughts were filled with worries for poor Chocky.

As the road levelled out, Mandy could hear the river running close by. It sounded deliciously cool and inviting. 'Let's dip Chocky's towel in the water,' she suggested. 'We'll need it to be nice and damp when we find her.'

'Good idea,' said James. 'Maybe we could have a bit of a rest, too.' He looked like he was feeling the heat as much as Mandy was. 'It's really humid. What we need is a thunderstorm.'

'That's not what Chocky needs,' Mandy reminded him. She glanced up at the sky, where dark-edged clouds were starting to gather ominously.

'It looks like we might be getting one anyway,' said James.

They parked their bikes and headed for the grassy river bank. Dillon said nothing. He'd been silent since they'd left Woodbridge Farm Park.

'Are you still worried about Gary?' Mandy asked him gently.

'Well, it looks bad for him, doesn't it?' said Dillon. 'I mean, no one saw him on Black Tor. We've only got his word for it.'

'Why don't you check through his clothes at home?' suggested James. 'If none of them have any paint stains, then you'll know he didn't do it.'

'I'm not going through his stuff like he's a criminal!' Dillon snapped. 'If he says he wasn't there last night, then that's enough for me.'

James blushed. 'It was just an idea.'

Mandy sighed. 'Dillon, James didn't mean to upset you. He was only trying to–'

'Help!'

Mandy jumped in surprise as her sentence was finished for her by a desperate voice in the distance.

'Somebody help me!' came the cry again.

James pointed over the river to where the slate-grey turrets of Bleakfell Hall loomed above the trees. 'It must be Mrs Ponsonby!'

'Sam Western said Viking had been seen round here,' Mandy remembered. 'Come on!'

The three of them scrambled for their bikes, as a third call for help sounded from the direction of Bleakfell Hall.

Seven

Cycling furiously, Mandy led the way up the narrow road to Mrs Ponsonby's enormous house. The leafy sycamores that lined the drive were showing the first touches of autumn colour. As Mandy, James and Dillon flew along, several of the broad-fingered leaves floated down lazily about them.

Soon Bleakfell Hall came into sight. It was an imposing building, broad and square with elegant towers stretching up to the sky at each corner. Mandy brought her bike to a skidding halt on the gravelled drive. The oak-panelled front door to the house was open, and there, standing beside one of the pillars on the front steps, was Mrs Ponsonby. Her glasses were perched halfway down her large nose. Her mouth was wide open in shock, and her double chin wobbled alarmingly. Even her carefully styled hair was in disarray. Clamped under one arm was her spoilt Pekinese, Pandora, who was looking up at her owner as if wondering what all the fuss was about.

'What's wrong, Mrs Ponsonby?' asked Mandy, panting for breath.

'In the garden!' she wailed. 'It's in the back garden, eating my bird table!'

'Er, what is?' asked James.

'A goat!' shrieked Mrs Ponsonby.

'Viking!' said Mandy with relief.

'My housekeeper is trying to shoo it away,' Mrs Ponsonby continued. 'But the beastly thing doesn't seem to care!' She pushed her spectacles back up her nose, then shook her head so they fell down again. 'I can't bear to look!'

'Shall we go and help?' Mandy offered politely. 'The goat's no trouble really. He escaped from

Woodbridge Park Farm last night after the place was vandalised, and we're trying to get all the animals back again.'

'You haven't seen a large guinea-pig around here too, have you?' added Dillon hopefully.

'A guinea-pig?' Mrs Ponsonby looked at Dillon and Mandy as if they were both quite mad. Then her face softened a little. 'Oh dear. I'm very sorry to hear about the farm but the only thing I've seen is that wretched goat. It's eating my private property and upsetting my little Toby! He's barking like a maniac through the French windows!'

Mandy smiled as she pictured Mrs Ponsonby's other dog, an affectionate mongrel. Mrs Ponsonby adored her pets but she did tend to worry too much about their health, often taking them to Animal Ark for a check-up when there was absolutely nothing wrong.

'If Mrs Ponsonby telephones the farm, they could come and collect Viking,' James suggested.

'But everyone will be outside clearing up,' Mandy reminded him. 'It might be hours before they get the message.'

'I'll go back and tell them on my bike,' said Dillon. 'I'll be as quick as I can.'

'All right,' Mandy agreed. 'James, let's see what Viking's up to!'

As Dillon pedalled frantically away, Mrs Ponsonby pointed to the dark green door in the wall that surrounded Bleakfell Hall's gardens. 'The goat got in through there. But be careful, won't you - he's a menace!'

Mandy and James tried to hide their smiles as they crossed quickly to the door and pushed through into Mrs Ponsonby's huge garden. Smooth green lawns stretched away to the woods at the bottom. It was at least twice the size of Viking's paddock. Mandy remembered the problems she and her father had experienced trying to corner Viking back at the farm, and she looked nervously at James. With trees, a pond and several statues to hide behind, Mandy doubted if the Angora goat would be any easier to catch here.

'Stop that, you rascal!' came an angry shout from Anna, Mrs Ponsonby's housekeeper. Viking was skipping joyfully about the garden with Anna in frantic pursuit. Occasionally he paused to let

Anna come teasingly close, but just as she was about to grab him he skittered off again, churning up mud from the flowerbeds with his hooves. From the French windows, Mandy could hear the frantic yelping of Toby, who was obviously desperate to join in the fun.

'Whoops,' said James, shielding his eyes with one hand. 'I can see why Mrs Ponsonby got upset!'

Mandy followed his gaze, and saw the well-chewed remains of what had clearly been a beautiful ornamental bird table. 'Oh dear,' she said as she crossed the hoof-marked lawn to inspect it. 'But Viking didn't do it on purpose,' she argued. 'He was just trying to get to the food Anna had put inside!'

'I don't suppose that'll make Mrs Ponsonby feel much better,' James pointed out.

Mandy nodded. 'Well, let's stop him before he causes any more trouble!'

'What are you two doing here?' called Anna. The little woman was red in the face from her exertions, and she looked far from pleased to see them.

'Mrs Ponsonby sent us,' Mandy explained.

'We're here to help you catch Viking. If we can lure him into a corner, we can hold him until his owners arrive.'

Viking bleated nervously when he saw Mandy and James fanning out to approach him from the opposite direction to Anna. He swung his shaggy head towards each of them in turn.

'Steady,' James advised Mandy and Anna as they began to close in on the suspicious goat. 'Not too fast, or we'll scare him . . .'

Too late. With a loud bleat Viking raced for the gap between Mandy and James. They lunged for him, missed, and ended up in a heap on the lawn. The goat quickened his step and headed straight for the washing line which was weighed down with several freshly washed items from Mrs Ponsonby's wardrobe.

'Now he's going to eat the laundry!' Anna squealed in panic.

But Viking seemed oblivious to the obstacle in his path and hurtled into the washing line like a marathon runner at the finishing line. His horns caught on one of Mrs Ponsonby's brightly coloured floral dresses. There was a loud snap as

he jerked the dress right off the line, sending the clothes pegs flying into the air. The material flopped down and covered Viking's entire head. At once he came to a halt, bleating in confusion.

'That's Mrs Ponsonby's best summer dress,' cried Anna.

'Perhaps you could put it back on the line before she notices,' James suggested, struggling to keep a straight face.

Mandy had to stifle her own laughter at the sight of the goat standing uncertainly with the flowery outfit draped over his head. He'd be easy to catch now.

'I think I'd better rescue that dress,' said Anna at last, bursting into giggles. 'I don't think Mrs Ponsonby would want to be seen in the same outfit as a goat!'

Once the dress was lifted from his head, Viking came quietly with Mandy and James. While Anna went back indoors through the French windows, Mandy gently steered the goat through the door in the wall and round to the front of the house. Mrs Ponsonby gave a shrill cry of alarm and retreated up the stone steps to her front door.

'It's all right,' Mandy told her. 'I think Anna wore him out!'

Before she could reassure Mrs Ponsonby any more, a tooting horn made her jump. With a sigh of relief Mandy saw Gary Lewis's battered van trundling up the driveway. Dillon was riding alongside it on his bike.

'How did you get to the farm so quickly?' asked James, sounding impressed.

'I didn't,' grinned Dillon. 'I met Gary coming the other way down the hill, going to fetch the things he needs for the hen houses.'

The van came to a halt in front of them, looking out of place in such well-tended surroundings. Mrs Ponsonby watched in dismay as Gary, with his scruffy clothes and unruly ponytail, guided the unprotesting Viking into the back of his van.

Mandy felt concerned when the goat had to duck his head to squeeze in. 'Will he be all right in there?'

'There's not far to go,' Gary told her. 'Ordinarily I'd walk him back, but it looks like there's rain on the way. Goats aren't as robust as sheep or cows and it's not good for them to be outside in the wet.'

Pandora, still wedged firmly under Mrs Ponsonby's arm, suddenly gave a loud yelp.

'All this excitement is bad for my poor darling!' announced Mrs Ponsonby, as Pandora barked again, struggling to be free. 'Now you've caught your silly animal, I'd like you to leave us in peace.' She had to raise her voice over her little dog's noisy yapping. 'And I'm afraid I shall have to bill Mr Woodbridge for the damage to my bird-table . . .'

But Mandy wasn't listening to Mrs Ponsonby any more. She was studying Pandora, still wriggling in her owner's firm grip. 'What is it, girl?' she asked. 'What's wrong?'

'There!' cried James, looking where the little dog's snub nose was pointing. 'Behind that urn. It's a rabbit!'

'Gracious!' Mrs Ponsonby stared at the rabbit in surprise.

'It's Springer,' said Dillon.

'Well done, Pandora!' laughed James as Dillon crunched across the gravel and carefully scooped up the black and white rabbit from its hiding place.

'Is she OK?' Mandy asked anxiously.

Dillon inspected the rabbit closely, and grinned at Mandy. 'She seems fine!'

'There's an old cardboard box in the back,' said Gary. 'I can empty it out, but I've got no straw to line it with.'

Mrs Ponsonby cleared her throat. 'I might be able to help there,' she said. 'Anna,' she called into the house, 'could you come here, please?' She turned back to Mandy. 'I've got a good deal of bedding in the house for my gerbil. You can borrow some of that.'

Mandy beamed. 'That's brilliant, Mrs Ponsonby! Thanks!'

'In that case, Mrs Ponsonby,' said Dillon quickly, 'would it be possible to borrow your gerbil's food bowl?'

'I have a spare as it happens,' said Mrs Ponsonby. 'But what on earth for?'

'Yes, why?' Mandy wondered.

'It could help us find Chocky,' said Dillon mysteriously.

Just then, Anna appeared, and Mrs Ponsonby sent her off to fetch the gerbil's bedding and the spare food bowl.

'Chocky?' repeated Mrs Ponsonby. 'Tel me, Mandy, how many other refugees might I find on my land?'

'Just that one,' said Mandy. 'Chocky's a pregnant guinea-pig. Her babies could be due at any time!'

'If we don't find her soon they could all be in real trouble,' James added solemnly.

Anna soon returned with the bowl and the bedding. Gary placed the hay in the box, and Dillon put Springer on to his temporary bed. He scampered around a few times, flattening the hay down, then started chewing on some fragrant stalks. To Mandy's surprise, Anna even sneaked a little bundle of hay to Viking in the back of the van. The goat munched it up quickly, blinking his bright eyes at Anna as if to say thank you.

'I won't tell if you won't,' Anna whispered to Mandy with a smile. 'That goat's given me the most fun I've had in ten years!'

* * *

With Springer's cardboard box wedged securely in the footwell of the passenger seat, Gary set off for the farm. Mandy, James and Dillon waved goodbye to Mrs Ponsonby and Anna and set off back down the drive.

'We must be on the right track,' said James. 'If Springer made it this far, so could Chocky. She could even have made it all the way to the village.'

'Why did you want the gerbil's food dish, Dillon?' Mandy asked.

'Do you still have that dried food you took from Pets' Corner?' he said.

Mandy dug into her jeans pocket and showed him the handful of seeds and cereal. Dillon held out the metal bowl so she could pour the food into it. The dried food rattled round with a loud clatter.

'Oh, I get it,' said James, his eyes widening. 'If we rattle the food in the dish, it might bring Chocky out of hiding!'

'It's just an idea,' shrugged Dillon.

'It's a great idea,' Mandy told him. 'Let's hope it works!'

As they renewed the search, their spirits were

high. Luck had been on their side, and they had found Viking and Springer. The only animal still missing was Chocky. Mandy was certain that with Dillon's good idea to help them, it wouldn't be long before Chocky was safely back at Woodbridge Farm Park.

But by lunchtime, although they had covered a lot of ground, and rattled the food dish until their ears rung, there was still no sign of Chocky.

The sky had continued to darken with gathering storm clouds, although the weather remained oppressively hot. Mandy felt hungry and thirsty, but she didn't want to waste a moment on lunch.

'I'm so hungry I could eat that guinea-pig food!' James sighed.

'Me too,' Mandy remarked gloomily. She looked up at the sky. 'It looks like it's going to start pouring any moment now.'

'At least that will cool us down,' Dillon pointed out.

They went on searching. Mandy was almost afraid to look in the roads in case Chocky had been hit by a car. But at the end of another hour crawling round the village green on hands and knees, rattling the food in the dish, there was still no sign of Chocky.

'In a way, no news is good news,' said James, trying to be positive. 'At least we know she hasn't been run over or anything.'

'Do we?' Dillon said bitterly. 'We've crawled along hedgerows, peered under trees, knocked on front doors and asked if we can search people's gardens, but there's just no sign of her. We don't know if she's dead or alive!'

'That's true,' Mandy admitted. 'We just don't know. And while we don't know, we have to go on looking.' She felt a lump building in her throat. 'Just in case.'

But even as she spoke, the inevitable happened. A low, menacing roll of thunder echoed around the heavy grey sky. Moments later, Mandy felt a large warm raindrop plop on to the back of her hand. Then another on her head. 'Oh no,' she whispered. 'The storm is starting!' She picked up her bike, and James and Dillon did the same.

'We can shelter at the church!' she yelled. 'It's not far!'

They leaped on to their bikes and tried to outrace the rain. But it started coming down in torrents, pelting against them as hard as hail. By the time they crowded under the lych-gate outside the church, they were all soaked to the skin.

'I hope Chocky's found some cover!' said James. He looked down at the food in the bowl, which the rain had turned to sticky mush.

'I'm sure she has,' Mandy said with a confidence she no longer really felt. 'The rain will soon pass. Then we can start looking again.'

Dillon said nothing, but stared sullenly out from their shelter at the deserted road. The temperature had dipped quite steeply with the breaking of the storm, and Mandy found she was starting to shiver. The rain kept up, and the thunder grew louder. Flashes of lightning lit up the graveyard.

'Hold on, Chocky, wherever you are,' Mandy murmured.

After what felt like ages, Mandy saw a familiar car pull up outside the church. Emily Hope unwound the window and peered out into the downpour.

'Mum!' Mandy yelled. 'What are you doing

here?'

'I'm on my way to pick up some waterproofs for your dad and me,' she called. 'I thought I'd find you three roaming about. This weather's all we need, isn't it? Any luck with Chocky?'

Mandy shook her head.

Mrs Hope pulled a face. 'I'm sorry, love. Look at you all, you're soaked through. Come on, jump in with me. I'm taking you home. You can put your bikes in the back.'

'But, Mum, we can't just give up!' Mandy protested.

'And you can't keep on looking in weather like this,' said Emily Hope. 'I know how important it is to find Chocky, but your health is important too. None of you will help her by catching a chill.'

Mandy bit her lip in frustration. 'Yes, but Mum–'

'And it just isn't practical to keep on searching in this rain, Mandy. When it stops, and when you've changed into some dry clothes, you can go out looking again, OK?'

Mandy hesitated. She wanted to keep on

looking, but deep down she knew her mum was right.

James pushed his dripping fringe off his forehead. 'We've done our best,' he reminded Mandy.

Dillon nodded. 'I guess all we can do now is hope Chocky's found somewhere safe and dry to shelter.'

Miserably, Mandy wheeled her bike over to the Land-rover, and James and Dillon followed on behind. As she climbed in she took one more look round the empty street. 'Don't worry, Chocky,' she murmured. 'We'll find you, I promise!'

Eight

The rain didn't let up all afternoon. Once they'd dried off, Mandy, Dillon and James tried playing board games to pass the time, but they couldn't concentrate. Giving up, they stared out of the window at the rain in glum silence. Around six o'clock, Gary called by to collect Dillon and offer James a lift home.

'We'll start looking again tomorrow morning,' James promised. 'First thing.'

Mandy nodded and forced a smile even though she felt like crying. 'First thing,' she agreed.

The front door closed behind them with a hollow click. Mandy returned to the kitchen window. A flash of lightning sparked through the dark grey clouds, and the rain drummed against the glass as heavily as ever. Mandy bit her lip. What chance did Chocky have in weather like this?

Mandy's parents came home not long after Gary had collected James and Dillon. They looked worn out.

'Goodness,' said Adam Hope, making a big show of wiping his brow and collapsing into a kitchen chair. 'I've not worked as hard as that in a long time!'

'How is everything at the farm?' Mandy asked.

'Everything seemed pretty much under control until it started raining,' her mum answered, making a beeline for the kettle and filling it with water. 'The most important thing is, all the animals are back where they belong.' She paused awkwardly. 'Almost all of them, anyway. I'm sorry about Chocky, Mandy.'

Mandy felt a lump in her throat as she fetched three mugs and dropped a teabag in each. 'As soon as it stops raining, I'm going back outside to look for her,' Mandy told them determinedly.

'Good idea,' said Mrs Hope.

Mandy looked at her mum, a bit surprised by her enthusiasm. 'You think there's still a chance of finding her safe and sound, then?'

Mrs Hope poured some milk into each of the mugs and nodded her head fiercely. 'There's always a chance, Mandy. And I'm proud of you for not giving up,' she said, passing Adam Hope and Mandy a cup of tea.

Mr Hope raised his steaming mug in a toast. 'Here's to never giving up.'

'To never giving up,' Mandy and her mother echoed solemnly.

The three of them stared out the window at the storm-swept landscape as they sipped their tea.

Mandy plonked her mug back down on the kitchen table impatiently. 'Won't this rain *ever* stop?'

'Cheer up, love,' said Mandy's mum. 'We're going round to your gran and grandad's soon. It seems Grandma overestimated how many sandwiches the volunteers would get through today. They need some help finishing them off!'

Mandy's stomach rumbled. She'd forgotten that she'd missed lunch. 'That'll be great,' she said. Besides, anything that helped to take her mind off Chocky for a while was a good thing.

It wasn't far to Lilac Cottage, where Mandy's grandparents lived, but the storm was still so bad that Mr Hope decided they should take the car. The rain rattled down on the roof of the Land-rover as they drove along. Mandy's dad switched the windscreen wipers on to their fastest setting, but still the world outside the car seemed little more than a melting blur behind the torrents of water.

Soon they were pulling up outside the house. Mandy sprinted through the garden and flung open the door. Her parents were right behind her, and all three huddled dripping in the hallway.

Grandma Hope came bustling out to meet them with a warm smile. 'It's not letting up, is it?' she tutted. 'Never mind, come through to the kitchen.' She squeezed Mandy's hand. 'I'd sooner you dripped on the tiles than on the hall carpet!'

Grandma's kitchen was spotless as usual. Mandy

and her parents took off their coats and hung them on the gleaming brass coat hooks mounted on the whitewashed walls. The cheery red gingham curtains were closed against the storm, and a jug of home-made lemonade sat on the pine worktop next to five tall glasses. 'I know it's not quite the weather for cold drinks,' said Gran as she started pouring. 'But since we've all been at it so hard today I thought we'd have worked up a thirst.'

'And an appetite too,' Mandy added, eyeing the huge plate of sandwiches on the kitchen table.

Mr Hope peeled back the clingfilm covering the sandwiches and helped himself. 'Where's Dad?' he asked through a mouthful of cheese and pickle.

'Out in his greenhouse, would you believe it?' said Gran. She rolled her eyes and smiled.

'In weather like this?' Emily Hope asked in surprise.

'He'd planned to have a good potter about in there today,' Mandy's gran explained. 'Now the work at the farm has been rained off he's decided to make up for lost time!'

'I suppose it's dry enough in there,' Mandy said. She slipped her coat back on and took a couple of large cheese and salad sandwiches. 'I'll go and say hello and take him these.' She stepped through the back door into the driving rain, crossed the garden and then splashed through the shallow puddles on the path that led to her grandad's greenhouse. An electric lantern glowed mistily through the glass, lighting her way.

The door stood slightly open, and Grandad Hope looked up from the plant he was tending and grinned at Mandy. 'Hello there,' he said, putting down his watering can. 'Come to give me a hand?'

'Come to give you a sandwich,' Mandy joked, holding out her slightly soggy offering. She tried to shut the door after her, but it grated against the paving and stuck open. A gust of wind splashed rain over the back of Mandy's neck and she winced.

'The door's a bit sticky, I'm afraid,' Grandad explained. He took a mouthful of sandwich, and a cucumber slice slipped out on to the soil-scattered floor.

Mandy surveyed her grandad's gardening hideaway. A workbench stretched along one glass wall, and beneath it were a number of odd-looking plants in plastic containers. Some were a mass of spindly tendrils, while others had broad, rubbery leaves. Pillow-sized sacks of fertiliser lay amongst them. The top of the workbench was cluttered with flower pots and seed trays, faded gardening magazines, pairs of secateurs and well-worn gloves. On the other side of the greenhouse, healthy-looking tomato plants in yellow sacks of compost braced themselves against their supporting poles, their fruit red and shiny.

Grandad Hope noticed Mandy admiring them. 'They're looking quite good, aren't they?' he said modestly. 'They don't taste bad either,' he added, waving his salad sandwich.

'Did you grow the cucumber as well?' Mandy asked, pointing towards the floor.

Grandad Hope looked at his feet in confusion. 'Eh?'

Mandy looked down. The cucumber slice had gone. 'It was there a moment ago,' she said, puzzled.

Her grandad shrugged. 'I must've kicked it out of the way.'

Mandy nodded.

At that moment, she heard a tiny high-pitched squeak. It sounded just like a guinea-pig. Chocky . . . the disappearing cucumber . . . could it be?

Grandad Hope looked at her in surprise. 'What on earth was that?'

'It sounded like . . .' Mandy dropped to her knees and stared round frantically. The concrete floor was cold and hard but she barely noticed. Desperately she started to heave the plants out of the way, ignoring her grandad's worried protests. 'It sounded like . . .' she said again, her heart in her mouth, unable to bring herself to finish the sentence. But finally she caught a glimpse of movement behind one of the sacks of fertiliser. A beady black eye gleamed in the dim electric light, and a furry brown and white shape shifted to one side.

'*Chocky*!'

It was all Mandy could do to stop herself shouting for joy and giving the guinea-pig an

enormous hug. But she knew that Chocky could be injured, and that to move her, especially while heavily pregnant, might be dangerous. Once she'd shoved the third plant to one side, its glossy leaves rustling madly, Mandy could clearly see the lost guinea-pig. She was sitting on some spilled potting compost. The cucumber slice lay at Chocky's feet, and she looked completely bedraggled, her fur wet and matted. And to Mandy's concerned eyes her abdomen seemed even more swollen than yesterday.

'She got all the way here,' Mandy marvelled softly.

'I'll fetch your mum and dad,' offered Grandad Hope. The door scraped loudly behind him, and Chocky twitched in alarm.

'It's all right, Chocky,' Mandy whispered, her eyes filling with happy tears. 'You're safe now!'

Chocky gave another piercing cry, making Mandy jump. It was louder than any noise she had ever heard from a guinea-pig.

Footsteps on the paving outside made Mandy look round with relief. Her mum was inside the greenhouse in a moment, while Grandad and Grandma Hope stood outside with an umbrella.

'Could one of you fetch us some more light, please?' Emily Hope asked calmly, crouching down to study the distressed guinea-pig.

'I'll fetch a torch,' said Gran. The wind caught her umbrella, nearly blowing it inside out, and she was propelled towards the house with a startled whoop.

Chocky shifted uncomfortably on the heap of compost.

'Did you hear that noise she made just before

you came in?' Mandy asked her mum.'Is she hurt?'

'Believe it or not, every pregnant guinea-pig makes that noise just once,' said Mrs Hope. 'It means she's about to give birth. Mandy, you found her in the nick of time.'

Mandy stared at her mum wide-eyed. 'But she looks exhausted. She must've been running all day! Chocky will be all right, won't she?'

Emily Hope didn't reply for a moment.'I don't know, Mandy,' she said at last. 'She's very stressed, probably hungry, and her body temperature must be quite low. I'm afraid it's going to be touch-and-go.'

'Where's Dad?' Mandy croaked, her mouth suddenly dry.

'He's dashed home to get some oxytocin to help Chocky's labour,' said Emily Hope, gently feeling round the guinea-pig's swollen hindquarters. 'We guessed she would be pretty close to having her babies. And she'll need all the help she can get.'

As if to confirm the diagnosis, Chocky started wriggling about more urgently.

'Mum, I don't think she's going to wait for Dad to get here!' Mandy whispered in alarm.

Mrs Hope nodded. 'Then we'll just have to help her ourselves.'

A beam of bright light fell into the greenhouse. The leaves of the plants scattered thick, sinister shadows around them. Mandy turned to see her grandma brandishing a heavy black torch in triumph.

'Shine it over here, please,' said Emily Hope. She pulled off her woollen jumper and arranged it on the dirty floor against one of the full sacks of fertiliser.

'You're making a nest for Chocky,' Mandy realised.

Her mum nodded. 'I've got another errand for you, if you don't mind,' she called to Grandma Hope as she patted down the jumper. 'I'll need a hot-water bottle, please, and some towels.'

'On my way,' said Gran. She passed the torch to her husband, and vanished again down the path.

Now Mrs Hope gently placed both hands underneath Chocky and edged her round on to the soft fabric so her back end was facing them. 'It's easier for us to see what we're doing,' she explained to Mandy, 'and the light won't shine straight in her eyes.'

'Look,' breathed Mandy, as Grandad Hope took the torch and trained it over Mandy's shoulder directly on to Chocky.

A tiny head was protruding from the mass of fur. A transparent filmy coating was stretched over it.

'Is that normal?' Mandy asked anxiously.

Her mum nodded. Mandy watched as the baby guinea-pig's pink nose broke through and twitched, breathing in air for the first time. Chocky's sides heaved and the baby slipped out on to the jumper.

'Good girl, Chocky!' whispered Mrs Hope. 'You're doing fine!'

The new baby squeaked with a tiny piping noise, and pushed itself up on to its paws. It sniffed the air, its black eyes beady and bright. Then it waddled off unsteadily to snuggle under its mother, worming its head around as it searched for milk.

'Mum, here comes another one!' Mandy said, biting her lip with excitement.

But Chocky seemed exhausted by her efforts with her first born. Her head lolled and her breathing was quick and shallow.

'Don't give up, Chocky,' Mandy muttered. She longed to stroke Chocky to give her comfort, but she knew it was best to leave her alone as much as possible.

At last the baby was born. It peered about through sleepy eyes, and gave a little cough.

'Is it all right?' Mandy asked anxiously.

'Actually, that's a good sign,' said her mum. 'It means the little one's airways are clear.'

The tiny guinea-pig soon smelled its mother and crawled over to be with her. Chocky weakly raised her head and licked half-heartedly at her second baby.

'Goodness me,' said Grandad Hope.

Mandy jumped at her grandfather's voice. She'd forgotten he was still hovering behind them. 'Is that another one on the way?' he asked.

'It certainly is,' said Mrs Hope as a third baby guinea-pig slithered out. But Chocky, still nudging and murmuring to the second baby, seemed not to notice. The third baby lay very still, not breathing.

'Looks like Chocky needs a midwife,' muttered Mrs Hope. She cupped the baby guinea-pig in both hands with its head towards her fingertips and swung it back and forth. 'If its membrane's not broken when it leaves its mother's body, the guinea-pig suffocates,' she explained.

'I've brought the hot-water bottle,' Grandma Hope called over to them. She looked drenched, but her eyes were shining with excitement.

'Wrap it in the towels and pass it to Mandy,' instructed Mrs Hope.

Mandy took the warming bottle. 'Shall I put it beside Chocky?' she asked.

Mrs Hope nodded, and Mandy placed the hot-water bottle against Chocky's rosetted fur. 'Here you are,' she cooed softly. 'Good, brave girl.' But suddenly, Chocky started to wriggle about again, and gave a low trilling noise. 'Mum!' Mandy called in alarm. 'I think there's another baby coming.'

Mrs Hope looked over, distracted. She had placed the lifeless guinea-pig down on its back and was pedalling its back legs with her fingers. 'Hang on, love. We have to get this one's airways open.'

Mandy bit her lip, still staring at Chocky. 'Mum, I think something's wrong . . .'

There was a tiny gasp from the guinea-pig in Mrs Hope's hands. Abruptly it twitched its head from side to side, instinctively looking for its mother.

'Good little fellow,' murmured Grandad Hope appreciatively.

'Quick, love, take over,' said Mrs Hope, passing the baby carefully into Mandy's trembling hands. 'Keep your hands cupped round it for warmth, and dry its fur on one of the towels.' She looked up at Grandma Hope. 'Could you fetch some milk, please? Mix it with a little water and warm it in the microwave.'

'I'll be right back,' panted Gran, turning away into the darkness.

'Oh dear,' murmured Emily Hope, studying the struggling mother. 'Looks like Chocky's got a breech birth on the way.'

'A breech birth?' gasped Mandy, staring into her mother's green eyes. 'Isn't that dangerous?'

'Very.' Emily Hope slid her hands underneath Chocky, and began gently to massage the guinea-pig's belly in a circular motion. Chocky shivered and squeaked faintly, but otherwise lay still. Her two healthy babies squirmed at her side. 'There's a chance I can turn the baby around into the correct position,' Mandy's mum explained quietly.

For what seemed like an age, Mandy watched her mother patiently rub the guinea-pig's abdomen. Chocky gave some grumbling squeaks, but lay still. The little baby in Mandy's hand squeaked softly as if in response.

'He wants his mum,' Mandy whispered.

'Keep him away for a moment,' said Mrs Hope. 'She's barely coping with two, and with another on the way . . . Wait a minute.' She grinned round at Mandy. 'I think it's coming!'

But a few moments later, her face fell. The baby's nose came out just as its siblings' had, but it did not twitch, and the mouth did not open. The tiny animal, once it was out, lay very still in a fold of Mrs Hope's jumper. Chocky didn't even turn to look at it.

Emily Hope lifted the baby in one hand and placed it up on the worktop.

Mandy felt tears welling up inside her.

Mrs Hope squeezed her arm. 'There was nothing we could do, Mandy. It was stillborn.'

'At least she's had three healthy babies,' added Grandad Hope gently.

Mandy nodded, and a tear splashed down on to her hand. The baby guinea-pig squeaked, surprised by the sudden shower, and nuzzled her finger with its tiny nose. Mandy found herself smiling again.

'OK, Mandy,' said Mrs Hope. 'You may as well let that one join his siblings. Let Chocky get to know him.'

Mandy placed the baby down by its brothers. Chocky raised her head and licked at the little one, making low murmurs and squeaks.

'You'll be all right now,' Mandy told the baby shakily. She turned to her mum. 'But what about Chocky? She looks so tired.'

As she spoke she heard urgent footfalls splashing down the path outside. Her dad came rushing up to the greenhouse, soaked to the skin and out of breath. He squeezed past Grandad Hope and laid down the heavy medical kit on the floor. 'Have I missed all the action?' he puffed.

'I'm not sure,' said Emily Hope, looking closely at Chocky. 'So far we've got two boys and a girl.'

Mandy quickly told her dad what had been happening.

Mr Hope's face fell when he heard about the stillborn baby. 'That's a shame. But given how exhausted and stressed Chocky must be, it's a miracle she hasn't lost her entire litter.'

'Should we give her some oxytocin to help with her contractions?' broke in Mrs Hope. 'I think she's about to have her fifth!'

Mr Hope was already filling the syringe. He passed it to Emily Hope. Chocky grunted as she felt the needle. She shifted about uncomfortably and squeaked in protest.

'That should help a little,' murmured Mr Hope.

'I've got the milk you wanted,' called Grandma Hope from outside the greenhouse.

'Brilliant,' said Mrs Hope. 'Mandy, take Chocky's little ones and place them by the hot-water bottle. I think she's going to need all her strength for this last one.'

Mandy did as she was told. The three tiny

guinea-pigs wriggled in her grip. They were already looking around them with keen interest. Mandy marvelled at the way they were born with all their fur and their eyes open. 'What shall I do next?' she asked.

'Hang on a minute. I'll just add some glucose solution to this milk,' said Adam Hope. 'Then you can do some hand feeding.' That done, he passed her an eyedropper. 'Fill this up, and let the babies suck from it. Don't squeeze the milk into their mouths, they could choke. Let them drink at their own pace.'

Mandy nodded and carefully drew up a small amount of liquid into the dropper. The first baby sniffed the air, then worked its mouth round the glass. 'That's right,' Mandy said encouragingly. 'Drink it all down.'

Beside Mandy, her mum shifted to ease her cramped legs. 'Come on, Chocky,' said Mrs Hope softly.

'What's wrong?' Mandy asked, alarmed at her mum's tone.

'She's in trouble, I'm afraid. The baby's not coming out.'

'Will it be all right?' Mandy's voice was barely a whisper.

Mr Hope craned his neck to see more of what was going on. 'Emily, can you hook your fingernail on to the baby's teeth?' he suggested.

'Have a go, Mum,' said Mandy, throwing her a quick glance as she tried to interest the second guinea-pig baby in the dropper. 'Please.'

'Hold on,' said Mrs Hope. Mandy wasn't sure if she was telling the baby to grab her nail, or the rest of them to keep quiet and let her get on with her work.

'That's right,' breathed Mr Hope. 'It's coming!'

'Oh, I can see its head!' gasped Grandma Hope. She squeezed Grandad's arm in excitement, but he managed to keep the light steady, grinning from ear to ear.

Mandy felt excitement welling up inside her. 'Yes! It's almost there!'

'Got you!' said Mrs Hope in triumph as the baby slipped wriggling on to the warm woollen jumper. 'Another girl!'

Chocky turned round at once, livelier now, fussing over the last of her litter. The baby nuzzled up to her, eager to feed.

'You made it, Chocky,' Mandy whispered proudly.

Mrs Hope winked at her. 'Here's to never giving up.'

'The baby guinea-pigs seem happy with the dropper,' Mr Hope observed. 'And that's probably a good thing. Chocky's going to be very weak for a couple of days. She may not be able to handle such a big litter for the time being.'

Emily Hope nodded. 'And it'll be another four weeks before they can be weaned.'

'Where will they all stay?' wondered Grandad Hope. 'I mean, they're welcome to use my greenhouse, but with the door not closing properly . . .'

'It would get too hot in here anyway, during the day,' said Mandy's dad. 'But I don't advise we move her very far just yet. She's too weak.'

'How about the shed?' suggested Gran. 'That's safe enough, and cool too.'

'Perfect,' said Mrs Hope. 'We'll watch over them here for a while, and move them later this evening.'

'There's still one question that needs answering,' said Mandy.

Everyone looked at her expectantly.

She grinned. 'What are we going to call Chocky's babies?'

'Let me see now,' said Mr Hope, scratching his bearded chin. 'How about Lucky, Luckier, Even Luckier and Luckiest?'

'Dad!' Mandy protested. She thought for a moment. 'I know!' she declared. 'They were born in a greenhouse, so how about Pumpkin, Pepper, Carrot and Radish!'

'Splendid names,' chuckled Grandad. 'You know, I always thought *I* had the green fingers around here.' He smiled down at Chocky and her new family of guinea-pigs, then at Mandy and Mrs Hope. 'But I can see I'm not the only one who can help things to grow in this greenhouse!'

Nine

The next day, James and Dillon came round to Lilac Cottage to visit Chocky and her new family, now happily ensconced in Grandad's cool shed.

'I have to admit, I never thought I'd see Chocky again,' confessed Dillon. 'Especially with so many healthy babies!' Behind him, sunlight streamed in through the shed door. The weather had changed once more, and it was as if last night's storm had never happened.

'I never thought I'd get to see her at *all,*' James

put in solemnly. 'I guess Chocky's just an amazing guinea-pig!'

They looked down at Chocky and her brood in the cardboard box on Grandad Hope's workbench. The four babies were pressed up against Chocky's side, jostling in the soft, sweet-smelling hay. Chocky chewed contentedly on a fresh piece of groundsel which James had brought for her.

'She certainly *is* amazing,' Mandy agreed, straightening up from the far side of the shed. She was holding a saucer in her hands as if it were a silver platter. 'How many other guinea-pig families get special service from their own waitress?'

Dillon looked at the mush on the saucer and pulled a face. 'I'm not sure I'd want that to be served up to me!' he joked. 'What's in there?'

'Bran mixed with some brown bread and milk,' Mandy told him. 'Mum says the babies should start having the same food as their mum within two days of being born.'

'Rather them than me,' laughed James. 'I'm looking forward to that lunch with the Woodbridges!'

Mandy nodded. Mr and Mrs Woodbridge had been delighted to hear that Chocky was safe and well, and had insisted that Mr and Mrs Hope – and Chocky's special search party, Mandy, James and Dillon – come for a celebratory meal at the Fox and Goose.

'I can hardly believe we managed to find all the animals in the end,' said James.

'It's well worth celebrating, that's for sure!' Mandy agreed with an enormous smile.

'How long will Chocky have to stay here?' asked Dillon.

'Just a couple of days,' Mandy told him. 'Then she'll be well enough to go back to Pets' Corner.' She placed the dish in the box, and one of the little guinea-pigs scurried over to sniff the food in the saucer. 'Until then, the Grandad Hope Hotel seems to be suiting them nicely! Hey, did you tell Gary the good news about Chocky?' Mandy asked.

Dillon nodded. 'Yeah,' he said. 'He's really pleased.' He sounded distracted.

Mandy frowned at James. 'Is anything the matter, Dillon?' she asked gently.

'It's just you mentioning Gary,' said Dillon with a gloomy shrug. 'Everyone still thinks he had something to do with the trouble at the farm.'

'That's only gossip,' Mandy declared. 'PC Wilde will find who really did it.'

'I suppose so.' Dillon didn't sound convinced.

'Well,' said James. 'I guess we should get ready to go to lunch!'

Mandy nodded enthusiastically. Dillon followed them silently out of the shed, and into the brilliant sunshine. Mandy felt a pang of sympathy for him. It looked as if it was going to take a lot more for Dillon to be satisfied that everyone believed in his brother's innocence.

The first thing Mandy saw as her parents' Land-rover pulled up outside the Fox and Goose was a very red-faced Sam Western, leaning under the open bonnet of his car. He seemed furious.

'Having problems?' asked Mr Hope.

'The wretched engine sounded bad before, but it's broken down completely now,' scowled Mr Western. 'I suppose I'll have to call out the garage. And on a Sunday, too! That'll cost me a fortune.'

'Should we offer him a drink?' wondered Emily Hope quietly.

'Perhaps we'd better not,' said Mr Hope. 'The mood he's in, he'd probably throw it at his car!'

Mandy, James and Dillon followed Mr and Mrs Hope into the Family Bar.

Julian Hardy, the landlord, welcomed them with a nod and a smile. 'Stuart called ahead to book the table,' he said. 'He says he and Mrs Woodbridge will be a bit late. They've got to wait at the farm for a delievery.'

'No problem.' Adam Hope ordered three lemonades, a mineral water and a pint of beer.

'Sorry, Adam,' Julian told him as the metal spout coughed and fizzed foam into the pint glass. 'Looks like I need to change the barrel. I won't be a moment.'

As Mr Hardy popped out to the cellar to sort out the new barrel, Mandy took a sip of her lemonade. 'How long can we leave Chocky and her babies together?' she asked her mum.

'Well, we should separate the boys from the girls after about six weeks,' replied Mrs Hope. 'The babies will be old enough to mate by the time they're eight to ten weeks, and we certainly don't want any more litters at this stage.'

Just then, they heard Julian Hardy's voice raised in anger from the beer garden. Two surly-looking youths, one short and one very tall and heavily built, burst into the Family Bar and crossed quickly to the front door. The tall boy almost knocked Mandy over.

'Are you all right?' asked James, reaching out to grab her arm.

Mandy opened her mouth to reply that she was fine, when the healthy roar of a powerful engine started up outside.

'It sounds like Mr Western's got his Land-rover going after all,' remarked Mr Hope.

Just then, Julian Hardy came back into the bar, a little red in the face. 'Sorry about that,' he said. 'I caught those two kids carving something into the cellar door.'

Mr Hope sympathised and paid for the round of drinks. As he was tucking his wallet back into his jacket, the front door opened and in walked Sam Western. Mandy was surprised to see that he was accompanied by Gary Lewis and Martin Tucker.

As the two boys entered, some of the people in the bar turned to stare. Mandy overheard one man say that Gary Lewis had a nerve showing his face anywhere in Welford. Now Mandy understood why Dillon had been so quiet earlier. As the whispers about his brother went on he looked downright miserable.

Sam Western, on the other hand, seemed very cheery. 'Young Martin here got my wretched Land-rover going,' he announced.

'It wasn't just me.' Martin gave an embarrassed grin. 'Gary lent a hand, too.'

Sam Western nodded. 'I can't believe it! I thought that breakdown was going to keep my vehicle off the road for ages.'

'No problem,' said Martin with a shrug. 'I've had to deal with far worse than that back in London.'

'Have you now?' said Sam Western thoughtfully. Then he cleared his throat. 'Well, let me buy you two lads a drink to say thank you.'

'Fine by me!' grinned Martin.

Gary nodded too, clearly taken aback by the change in Sam Western's manner. He gave Dillon a discreet thumbs-up. 'Tell you what, Dillon, we'll join you in the garden later.'

Dillon nodded and smiled.

'Come on, you lot,' said Mr Hope. 'Let's wait for the Woodbridges in the sunshine.'

Mandy led the way outside to the beer garden. There were lots of people there already, making the most of the summery weather. Only one table was free. As Mandy swung herself on to the warm wooden seat, her foot caught on something. Frowning, she peered down to see what it was. 'Someone's left their coat!' she exclaimed.

'It's a leather jacket,' James noted, sitting down beside her. 'That was probably quite expensive.'

'You'd better take it inside to Julian,' said Mrs Hope. 'I'm sure the owner will be back to collect it.'

Mandy lifted the heavy black coat. The back of the jacket was covered in metal studs, patches and logos. It must belong to one of the bikers, she thought as she walked back inside.

Gary, Martin and Sam Western were still at the bar with their drinks. Mandy stood beside them, resting the jacket on the bar. As she did so,

something caught her eye and she froze in shock.

The sleeve of the jacket, from the shoulder down to the elbow, was smeared with white paint.

'Is everything all right, Mandy?' asked Julian Hardy, looking over with concern. 'What have you got there?'

'I'm fine,' Mandy said breathlessly. 'I'm great! I've got *evidence*!'

'Evidence?' Baffled, Mr Hardy came over to see. 'Evidence of what?'

Mandy tapped the paint-covered sleeve and grinned over at Gary and Martin in triumph. 'Whoever wore this was at Woodbridge Park Farm two nights ago – there's a smear of paint on one of the barns that should match this perfectly!'

'Let's have a look,' said Martin curiously, picking up the jacket and unfolding it.

Gary pointed to a set of initials. 'B.B. That could be Brett Bowen. Did you see a tall bloke, a bit stocky?'

Mandy nodded. 'That sounds like the boy who pushed past me.'

'He's one of the Walton Wranglers, isn't he?' Gary asked Martin.

Martin nodded and pulled a face. 'Yeah, one of the new lads. Nasty piece of work, if you ask me. With people like him about, the gang's not the same as it used to be.'

'I'd say you're better off out of it,' said Sam Western firmly.

Martin sighed. 'I have to agree with you. Brett and a couple of the others were laughing about the way they drove through the Woodbridges' sheep the day before the farm got messed up. Said it had given them an idea for some fun.'

Mandy stared at him, wide-eyed. 'Do you think Brett was responsible for wrecking the farm?'

'After hearing that, and seeing this jacket, *I* do,' said Sam Western grimly, fishing his mobile phone from his pocket. 'And so will PC Wilde, I reckon. I'll give him a call right now. I know he's been talking to your gang, Martin, but without evidence there's been nothing more he can do.'

'Until now,' said Mandy quietly, gripping the thick black material with both hands.

Julian Hardy nodded solemnly. 'Brett Bowen might as well have signed his name in that paint!'

'And it looks like the two of you are definitely off the hook,' said Sam Western loudly, as if for the benefit of everyone in the Fox and Goose.

Gary and Martin went red, but Mandy guessed they were really pleased. 'I can't wait till Mr and Mrs Woodbridge get here so we can tell them the good news,' she said, her eyes shining. 'This really *will* be a celebration dinner!'

Ten

'It looks amazing!' Mandy gasped.

She, James and Dillon stared in disbelief at the courtyard. Last time Mandy had been at the farm, the whole place was a mess. Now it looked like a show farm. The paint on the barn walls had been scrubbed off. The barn doors had been newly decorated in bright colours. The cobblestones gleamed, still slick with water from the hose. A group of chickens scratched contentedly in the dusty ground outside their restored hen house.

'The whole farm's better than ever!' declared James.

'How did you do all this so fast, Mrs Woodbridge?' Mandy asked.

'We had half the village helping us, thanks to your grandparents,' Mrs Woodbridge chuckled. 'It's wonderful what can be done when everyone pulls together. The insurers came out to assess the damage on the first day, so we could get straight on with fixing everything.'

'Chocky won't recognise the place!' beamed Dillon. He was carefully holding a cardboard box filled with straw. Mandy opened the flap at the top and looked down at Chocky and her babies. At four days old, Pepper, Carrot and Radish already looked like miniature versions of their mother, their tortoiseshell fur divided into perfect tiny rosettes. Only Pumpkin had smooth fur, the colour of warm caramel.

Mandy sighed, her heart heavy with mixed feelings. Last night, her dad had checked Chocky over and declared her fully recovered from her adventure. There was nothing to stop her going back to Pets' Corner now. So, this morning, Mr

Hope had dropped them off at Woodbridge Farm Park with Chocky and her babies to wish them all goodbye.

'I'll miss you,' Mandy murmured. The tiny animals scampered about in the box, while Chocky munched busily on a dandelion leaf. 'All of you.'

'Hey! Is that who I think it is in that box?' came a familiar voice.

Mandy looked up to see Gary Lewis leaning against the open barn door, a big smile on his face.

Mrs Woodbridge nodded. 'Chocky's come back to stay, with all her babies!'

'Thanks for bringing her, guys.' Gary smiled warmly at Mandy, James and Dillon. 'Hey, did you hear the good news?'

'What, about Brett Bowen and his two friends being charged with the vandalism?' Mandy nodded. 'Dad heard all about it from PC Wilde when he brought his dog in for a check-up yesterday.'

Gary grinned. 'If you hadn't found that jacket, Mandy, I bet people would still think I had something to do with it. But actually, there's more good news. I'm talking about Martin.'

'What about him?' asked Dillon.

'Sam Western was so pleased with the job he did on the Land-rover, he's had a word with a friend of his who owns a garage in Walton. Apparently the guy's looking for a mechanic, so Martin might get a job!'

'That's great! Fingers crossed,' Mandy said.

There was a burst of squeaking from the cardboard box. 'I think Chocky can tell she's home,' said Dillon. 'She must've really missed Abby.'

'I think Abby's missed Chocky, too,' Gary agreed. 'But she's been a bit distracted by her new home.'

'New home?' Mandy echoed.

'Come and see,' said Gary, leading the way inside the small animals' barn.

Mandy was pleased to find that all the hutches had been righted and repaired, and that the lanterns were hanging neatly on new hooks. There was no sign at all of the chaos left behind by the vandals. And in one corner of the barn, something very special had appeared.

'Wow!' exclaimed James. 'Look at that!'

One of the hutches was mounted on bricks in the centre of a miniature paddock. A wooden ramp sloped gently down from the hutch's living room into the spacious ground area, which was strewn with sawdust and fenced in by neatly sawn logs. Carrots, cabbage leaves and pieces of cucumber were littered around. As Mandy and her friends drew nearer, Abby looked up at them from a big bowl of dried food, chewing eagerly on a sunflower seed.

'I built this yesterday,' Gary explained. 'With four little ones to look after, I thought Chocky and Abby could do with a bit more room.'

'It's a perfect guinea-pig nursery!' Mandy declared.

'Let's see if they like it,' said Dillon.

Gently, Mandy scooped up Chocky while James and Dillon lifted out her babies.

'Off you go,' whispered Mandy, as she placed Chocky carefully beside Abby.

Immediately, Chocky began exploring her new home, trundling briskly through the sawdust and gazing around with keen interest. Pepper and Radish squeaked at Abby, who sniffed gently at the two youngsters. Pumpkin and Carrot trotted off to investigate the cool shadowy space underneath the hutch.

Looking very satisfied with her new surroundings, Chocky walked back over to Abby. Together, the two guinea-pigs started nibbling at opposite ends of the same cabbage leaf.

'She doesn't just *like* her new home,' smiled Dillon. 'She *loves* it!'

'And so do her babies,' James laughed.

Mandy laughed too. 'Good girl, Chocky,' she whispered. 'Welcome home.'

NGEON

ntings 1

y and James will do anything to help an animal in distress. And sometimes even ghostly animals appear to need their help . . .

Skelton Castle has always had a faithful deerhound to protect its family and grounds. But Aminta, the last of the line, died a short while ago. So when Mandy and James explore the creepy castle the last thing they expect to see is a deerhound – especially one which looks uncannily like Aminta . . . Could it possibly be her? And what does she want with Mandy and James?

Another Hodder Children's book

CAT IN THE CRYPT
Animal Ark Hauntings 2

Lucy Daniels

Mandy and James will do anything to help an animal in distress. And sometimes even ghostly animals appear to need their help . . .

Mandy is haunted by dreams of a mysterious cat. Could it be because she is worried about Bathsheba, the vicarage tabby who has run away? Or does the strange, stone-coloured cat of her dreams have something to tell her?

Another Hodder Children's book

STALLION IN THE STORM
Animal Ark Hauntings 3

Lucy Daniels

Mandy and James will do anything to help an animal in distress. And sometimes even ghostly animals appear to need their help . . .

Mandy and James can hardly wait to accompany her dad to Folan's Racing Stables. But they find that Folan's is in trouble. Some of the jockeys believe it's because the stables are haunted by Tibor, one of their stallions, who died in a race. Can Mandy and James discover the truth – and help Tibor make his peace?